THE LAST NIGHT IN AMSTERDAM

BY
MELANIE ATKINSON

CHAPTER ONE: JENNIFER

The backstage area of the theatre is cold and quiet. I am the only person here. The coordinator is long gone, having led me down the labyrinthine tunnels to wait here and then scarpered off to her, I assume, lovely light and warm office not in the bowels of this building. Rubbing my arms through the thin fabric of my suit jacket, against the chill, I peak through the heavy velvet curtain and watch the auditorium fill up with people who have come specifically to see me talk. Me! The idea of people buying tickets, spending actual money to listen to me seems absurd. But here I am. Soon dozens of pairs of eyes will be trained on me, listening to me give a talk based on the most horrific thing that has ever happened to me. My stomach clenches painfully and there is hot saliva in the back of my mouth, readying it for a cataclysmic ejection from my stomach. But there is nothing left. I've already thrown up the cup of coffee I had this morning, the only breakfast I could manage. Even the glass of water, hastily sucked down before checking (for the millionth time!) I had my keys, my phone, that my straighteners were cold and unplugged, the knobs of the oven were set to off, soon made its way noisily and splashily into the toilet bowl. I am empty.

To try and distract myself from my mutinous stomach I think about all the adages and advice I'd read when looking up tips for public speaking - talking to the back of the room, picking one member of the audience and speaking to them directly, imagining everyone in their underwear etc. The thought of all these people in their knickers and boxers forces a hysterical giggle up my raw throat and out into the dusty air. The sound technician rigging up the projector on stage looks back fearfully through the curtains at the weird expulsion of noise. I can't blame him. We're all a lot jumpier than we were a year ago and this backstage area is seriously creepy; tight and full of shadows. I've noted all the exits in my head at least twenty times, but I'm still jittery and starting to sweat through my blouse despite the cold. Wafting it away from my body, I can smell myself and it's making me even more anxious. Did I even put deodorant on this morning? I can't remember. Anxiety has turned my memory into a moth-eaten blanket, a patchy thing with holes big enough to lose whole objects. I am always looking for something lost, tangible things that were seemingly in my hand only a moment ago but which are then found hours later between sofa cushions, under my pillow or on the floor. The less tangible things have been much harder to find.

Once everyone has taken their seats, the

overhead lights go down and the stage is only illuminated by the footlights. The backstage area is plunged into near total darkness. My heart rate accelerates and my breath comes faster and faster. The sound of my panting is loud in the gloom. I am no longer comfortable in the dark. The electric bills for my flat have risen astronomically in the last year. I've also spent a considerable amount on torches and a whole drawer full of candles in case I run out of batteries. I've gone through packets and packets of them recently and I've still got no idea how to recycle them. There's a growing bag of them next to the kitchen bin with no destination in sight.

I dig my fingernails into the palms of my hands to steady my breathing. The sound technician barely has time to finish announcing my name before I'm striding out onto the stage, microphone in hand, desperate to be free of the shadows.

"Can we raise the house lights?" I ask the faceless darkness, cringing at the shrill note of panic that has crept into my voice.

As they come on, the whole auditorium is full of rapidly blinking faces, some gripping the arms of their seats, some laughing skittishly with each other, but most looking relieved.

"I don't know about you guys, but I'm not keen

on a big, dark room where I can't easily see the way out." This elicits a few nervous titters from the audience. Everyone knows what I'm talking about. Everyone agrees but doesn't want to admit it out loud. All of us are afraid of the dark. I am about to make them more afraid.

"Ladies and gentlemen, my name is Jennifer Sawson. I was one of the very few people who made it out of Amsterdam alive last year. I've come to speak to you tonight to explain how and what you can do to keep yourselves safe should you find yourself in a similar position."

Walking to the front of the stage, I try to concentrate on the sound of my heels ringing out on the polished wood instead of the multitude of eyes which track my progress. Taking a deep breath, I pick up the clicker from the little table that also holds a sweating glass of water and a box of tissues, courtesy of the organisers. The first slide clicks into place. The image, nearly four feet high, is of me on the day I left Amsterdam, taken by a soldier at the airport. One of my eyes is swollen shut, my hair is caked in old blood and sweat, my hands are bound tightly in swaths of gauze like an Egyptian mummy. My smile is wide and manic, showing too many teeth and starting to curl in on itself at the edges like burnt paper. I was smiling because I was alive. I'd made it out and the full horror of what I'd seen and done was only perched on my shoulder, arms around my neck like a pet monkey. It hadn't yet engulfed me with a year of screaming nightmares, flashbacks and paralysing survivor's guilt, trying to squeeze the life out of me.

With my own horrifying visage as a backdrop and the stares of the audience burning into me, I take one last deep breath and fall into the yawning pit of memories from last year and my ill-fated holiday in Amsterdam.

**

Booking a trip to Amsterdam had been the latest in a long line of schemes to try and beat the winter blues. I had hoped it would act as a small beacon in yet another unrelentingly dark, cold and wet London winter. Every year I dreaded it. As the crunchy autumn leaves turned slushy under my boots and I brought my thick woollen coat out of the wardrobe I could feel my mood plummet, turning as gloomy as the sky when I woke up and when I came home. Everything felt dark. I'd read every article and blog post that purported to have a sure fire way to beat the sadness that began creeping over me in November and didn't abate until spring was in full fling. I'd tried Vitamin D and St John's Wort tablets, spending an entire lunchtime perusing their properties, and those of their shelf mates, in the aisles of Holland & Barrett, spending a small fortune in the process. I'd tried bracing walks, forcing my well wrapped body around the scrabby park at the back of my building, leaving my face wind chapped and red which only served to irritate me further and to spend yet more money. This time on regenerating moisturiser. One evening, desperate not to have to look at my miserable face reflected back at me in the dark train window, I'd picked up a discarded Metro and read an article about SAD lights. It was a contraption that was meant to deliver a simulated burst of sunlight to trick my body into dumping feel good hormones into my blood stream. My phone told me expedited shipping would have one delivered to me the next day. Yet more money spent.

Clearing away a pile of half empty foundation bottles, crusty mascara wands and discarded tissues with lipstick kisses of various shades, I set the lamp up where I got ready every morning. Maybe it could be two birds with one stone situation – giving me the light needed to put on my face as well as cheering me up. Stupidly I stared directly at the lamp before flipping the switch. The resulting glare made me yowl like a cat whose tail had been stepped on. For a moment I was seriously concerned that I had burned two permanent sunspots into my retinas. It was as though I were being dazzled with the glare of my own sadness. Thankfully my vision cleared and the lamp was soon relegated back to its box and stuffed under the bed to wait past the returns deadline and muster with the rest of the junk under there that I did not want to deal with.

Finally, and most expensively of all, I decided a mini break would be the thing to solve my winter induced malady. I didn't have the money for a destination with actual winter sun but a slew of websites informed me, although cold, Amsterdam would be beautiful in the winter. Each one promised me light installations along the canals, boat trips and twinkly winter markets packed full of giddily smiling people holding steaming cups of Bisschopswijn. I was sold. I couldn't wait for a few days of lie-ins, rather than the sea of commuters I always found myself jostled along by, surging down the steps of Cannon Street station, avoiding hawkers of religion and newspapers to disperse into the busy, fume-filled streets of central London.

The flight was exceptionally early and I arrived at the airport at, what felt like, the very middle of the night. Still, it didn't stop me from making my way to the airport bar to sit amongst other bleary eyed travellers enjoying the first pint of their holiday. Apart from Christmas day, the first day of your holiday is the only socially acceptable time to have a drink before 10 a.m. However, it did mean I arrived in Amsterdam with an impressive haystack hairstyle from my comatosed nap against the airplane's window, a raging thirst and a headache that seemed to be filling my brain like builders' expanding foam. It didn't help matters that Schiphol airport is predominantly made of glass; a painfully bright place if your early morning drinking is rapidly becoming your early morning hangover. Cheating seemed the best option and so I booked an Uber rather than having to work out the train timetable or brace myself for the shuddering, juddering bus into town. The very thought of it made the massive amount of Toblerone I'd scoffed on the plane, before my impromptu nap, slosh perilously in my stomach. I bought a bottle of water in one of the kiosks and gulped at it lustily, noisily and quite frankly disgustingly while making my way outside. My appearance was that of someone who had just been rescued from the desert rather than a tired tourist who'd spent the last couple of hours stuffing chocolate and alcohol into her face at the crack of dawn.

A sigh of relief slipped from between my lips when the Uber pulled up outside the hotel. Having never booked a last minute holiday before, but having of course heard horror stories of people booking accommodation blind and ending up in backstreet dives with tourists vomiting outside their windows and cockroaches the size of small dogs scurrying over their exposed limbs at night, I was very glad to see the hotel looked exactly as it had online. It was picture perfect, exactly like those in the travel brochures for Amsterdam, wedged tightly against its neighbours in a higgledy piggledy line like bad teeth in a big smile. It stood right on the canal and I paused for a while at the water's edge, breathing in the brackish smell of the water and watching tourists wave from the decks of their boat tours. My headache was throbbing at the back of my skull but despite it I was glad to have fled dreary London, if only for a few days.

The man behind the desk in the hotel was pleasant, efficient and spoke better English than me. It always made me embarrassed that the only foreign language skills I had were a couple of phrases of primary school French which would only ever come in handy if someone asked me how I was, how to get to the library or the names of my family – *Bonjour! je m'appelle Jennifer! Où est la bibliothèque?* That and some creative insults in German - *Leck mich am Arsch!* The hotelier smiled and handed me a gold key with a wooden toggle bearing the number of my room. Of course there wasn't a lift. Standing at the bottom of the crazy winding staircase with my overly heavy suitcase I wondered if anyone would notice if I had a little nap on the landing. I was ominously and embarrassingly close to shedding a couple of petulant tears at having to drag my suitcase up the stairs by myself. Why hadn't I just brought I a holdall or even a roomy backpack? Instead I'd packed enough clothes for two weeks even though I was only staying a couple of nights. There was no reason at all to have brought sandals to a city full of cobbled streets in the middle of December but packing had never been my forte. I always doubled the amount of underwear that I'd normally wear at home, as though going on holiday made it more likely I would soil myself and need emergency back up pants.

I dragged the overloaded bag behind me up each step, swinging it wildly around the tight bends, taking chunks out of the walls and my own shins until I reached my room. It was smaller than I'd expected, though I'm not sure what I'd really thought I'd be getting in a skinny Amsterdam hotel at a knock down price. Perhaps I'd been spoilt by too many carbon copy chain hotels, but the bed looked springy at least and the bathroom clean. A cursory hair check around the toilet, sink and shower confirmed it free of stray intransigent pubes or massive spiders. A hot shower washed the travel off my skin and a couple of paracetamol made me more 'capable adult' and less 'crotchety child' even if I did have to wrestle with the built in hairdryer. I might have had a small wardrobe's worth of clothes but, of course, I'd forgotten my own hairdryer, straighteners and a plug adapter.

Ostensibly the predominant reason for my trip had been fleeing London with a side of culture and cuisine but the first place I decided to visit was a coffee-shop I'd found online. I based the majority of my life decisions on the opinions and star ratings of other people these days, and the reviews for the coffee-shop looked, on the whole, pretty good. There was also an illicit thrill in being able to engage overtly in an activity still illegal at home. Of course I'd partaken in a couple of little tokes at university parties when it was de rigueur but I'd never been a serious stoner unlike my flatmate who had always been carrying and whose clothing was always peppered with little blimmer holes from the rough hash she smoked. I looked her up on Facebook before leaving for Amsterdam. She was now a credit controller with a slick bob, a beige looking husband and a chubby toddler frequently pictured painted in a dazzling array of chocolate biscuits. She looked as though she'd turned out okay, the kind of person who probably has a skin care routine and a good stock portfolio. She certainly didn't look like someone with a problem, unless that problem was a propensity for kitschy 'Live. Laugh. Love' signs as part of their interior decor. A couple of joints on holiday wasn't going to hurt, I reasoned. It would be fun!

The coffee-shop was bright and open, full of lush, bushy plants, large crystals and Buddha statues. It looked mellow without being overtly hippy. It didn't look as though someone was going to engage me in a four hour discussion about the virtues of hemp. Making my way inside I smiled at the man at the counter, who didn't return it but waved his hand in a gesture I took to mean choose anywhere. There was a plastic laminated menu on each table detailing all the different blends and breeds with their characteristics; smells, tastes or types of high. It was as overwhelming as all of the flavour notes ascribed to highly priced wines on restaurant menus. There didn't seem to be a 'House' option for those who didn't understand the differences between hash, weed, hazes, widows or kushes. I had no clue, I'd just smoked whatever had been going around the room at university. Thankfully the server, who came over once I'd taken a seat, took pity and directed me to the mildest pre-rolled joint. I smiled gratefully and nodded my assent. The other menu on the table was for snacks, something I was infinitely more comfortable with. Ordering a hot chocolate I leaned back in my seat to enjoy a little people-watching out of the window. I did a little surreptitious people watching of those inside the cafe too. Thankfully it didn't look to be all tourists. To my right was a foursome playing cards and behind them a man struggling not to nod off over his newspaper. Of course there was at least one table of nervous looking tourists, like they were waiting for undercover police to jump out of the tall potted palms at any moment and take them into custody.

The man returned, bringing a conical, pre-rolled spliff and a small cellophane wrapped bag of sugared sweets.

"You haven't smoked before," a statement more than a question. "A little bit of sugar will help," he said, handing me the bag of sweets. "And go slow." He gestured to the unlit joint between my fingers.

Unsurprisingly, I did not in fact go slow. It's hard to do so when it's just you and you worry about wasting the joint you have just spent several euro on. The idea of stubbing it out part way through and saving the rest for later never entered my mind. It wasn't the way I consumed chocolate or crisps or wine. Moderation was just not in my nature.

Lighting the joint I sucked in the hot smoke and tried to hold it in my lungs for as long as possible without coughing and immediately identifying myself as a newbie tourist. Finally, I let the great plume of smoke out into the already fuggy air. It were as though I were blowing the remaining tension from the morning's travel (and the rest of my life) out from the very bottom of my lungs. A great, warm, weighted blanket seemed to fall over me. It was the most relaxed that I'd been in a very long time, probably for much of my adult life. My mind emptied of worries; had I packed enough, had I locked the hotel room door, had I done a proper hand over at work, had I left the stove on at home and on and on and on, released out into the smoke. The kind of worries that tickle the back of your mind every day were now just white noise and I understood why a lot of people tried to live their whole lives under the numbness of this chemical blanket. It was a feeling I could get used to. If I'd just knocked the cherry from the glowing tip and savoured the mellow high I probably would have been all right, but inexperience, hubris or, more likely, greediness led me to suck the entirety down in a pretty short space of time.

As the smouldering remains of my joint coughed out the last of its smoke in the ashtray I wrapped my hands around the warm hot chocolate mug and watched the outside world pass me by with a silly smile plastered on my even sillier face. It was probably the same goofy smile my room-mate always seemed to have whilst I grimaced over assignments. If only I'd taken a leaf out of her book, joining her on the beanbag that spilled its little polystyrene guts out every time you sat on it, in her weed fogged room and chilled out a bit more I might have had a better time at university rather than worrying over a degree which didn't seemed to have advanced my life one iota. I couldn't tell if it was because my brain was chemically slowed but everyone on the street looked to be moving at quite a clip down the canal path away from the coffee-shop. It was a weekday and although I might have been on holiday it was surprising to see so many people out on the street. Pondering this, I watched as the foursome exited and joined the throng of people making their way towards what I assumed was the centre of town, leaving me alone in the smoky room.

Deciding not to worry about it I let my mind bounce pleasantly from topic to topic, not lingering for long enough to let any worry bleed into the edges. I could have stayed like that all day had my bladder not issued a dull alert somewhere on the periphery of my consciousness. The cup of hot chocolate had gone right through me. Scanning the room I finally found the sign for the toilet at the other end of the counter but being able to move was a different matter entirely. I was implanted on the chair, like my legs had grown roots and seeped through the tiles of the floor and into the soft loam of the earth to reach past small pebbles and pearlescent pink worms to hold me fast in place.

Wiggling my toes experimentally, I'd half expected to feel soil between them and was disappointed when they only chafed against the rough material of my socks. Annoyingly the message from my bladder was becoming more insistent, battling its way through my clouded mind. There was a decision to be made.

The world tipped a little as I stood and a clammy sweat broke out on my forehead. My stomach clenched. This feeling was worse than being drunk. It were as though I could actually see my blood pressure dropping, like a giant cartoon thermometer plunging down with the sound of a slide whistle. I sat back down heavily. Easing the queasy hot feeling creeping over my entire body was much more important than alleviating my full bladder. The previous headache, once banished with painkillers, came roaring back into a prominent position at the front of my skull. As I stumbled back into the seat, my hand brushed the previously forgotten packet of sweets. I grasped at it, struggling with it with number fingers. Finally my nail tore a hole large enough to manoeuvre the contents onto my palm, the feat as difficult as anything from the *Krypton Factor*. Pushing a handful of the brightly coloured confections into my mouth I swirled them around with my tongue, my mouth moistening in reaction. The sweetness made my face contort into, what I assumed was, a very attractive gurn. Jagged crystals of sugar tumbled down my dessicated throat and hit my system like a sledgehammer. The cartoon thermometer in my mind begin to rise again. I would have kissed that man if I'd been able to see him properly. My vision was like an old VHS with bad tracking, skipping and sliding around the room.

The sugar from the sweets had taken away some of the immediate danger of pulling a whitey, but I still didn't feel good. It was obvious they were a temporary fix at best. Sweat was beginning to pool in my hairline and my stomach rolled unpleasantly. Worse than either of those things was 'The Fear'; the unnamed, unknowable sensation that everything is terrible and about to get more so, but you can't quite put your finger on why. It crept up my back like a serpent and coiled its tail around my neck, flicking its tongue against my clammy skin. I still needed to use the bathroom but the thought of being that lightweight who can't handle themselves and topples over ungraciously in a public place on the way was a serious turn off from even trying. I might have been a confident lone traveller but I wasn't confident enough to style that out. The cafe was suddenly too open, too exposed and not safe enough. I needed to get back to the room, somewhere cosy and enclosed where I could sleep off this dreadful state of consciousness. It didn't matter that I still needed to pee. There was plenty of packed underwear waiting in my hotel room if the worst happened.

Even though the hotel was embarrassingly close by I could not trust myself to walk back to it. There were too many uneven surfaces, actual open water and the possibility that I was going to pee myself in public. Closing one eye, in a desperate attempt to focus, I used my phone to book another Uber and resolutely crossed my legs until it arrived. My phone trilled on the table, alerting me that my driver had arrived. I knew that in my logical brain, but my fear was telling me once I touched the screen there would be a message from my boss telling me I'd been sacked, or from my mum telling me something terrible had happened or an ex-boyfriend telling me he had the clap. All of those scenarios were so terrifying that I simply didn't bother to look at the phone. Instead, stumbling and lurching my way from my seat and out of the coffee-shop, trying not to bump into anyone on the way, I made my way outside. There was a car waiting at the kerbside.

A group of teenagers from the increasing throng brushed past me on the pavement in their haste to get where everyone else seemed to be going. Their touch, however brief and light, made my whole body cringe. I was jangly and vulnerable, convinced something bad was about to happen. Reaching into my pocket I clasped the hotel key between my knuckles. The sober part of my brain coaxed my anxiety riddled body into the back of the car. I felt better, safer, after the door closed but the driver didn't look up from his phone.

The tinny vibrations of whatever he was watching reverberated around the car's interior as I struggled to click the seatbelt into place. Eventually, fully secured, I looked over, waiting for him to turn the key. Nothing happened. The man didn't say a word to me. Panic threatened to wash over me. I hadn't looked at the alert on my phone, hadn't checked the make and model of the car due to pick me up or the license plate. What if I'd gotten into the back of a stranger's car? What if he was going to take me to some unused ship yard on the outskirts of town and sell me to the highest bidder? What kind of stupid tourist gets into the back of a stranger's car in a different country when absolutely battered? It was the kind of thing you saw on the news, while you shook your head and exclaimed that you'd never put yourself into that kind of situation.

Finally the driver realised I was there.

"Sorry, het spijt me," he threw over his shoulder, placing his phone screen side up on the passenger seat next to me.

"You're not going to watch that while you drive are you?" I asked stickily, cotton-mouthed from the spliff.

"Nee. Sorry. I just..have you seen? Uh. Okay, don't worry. Your hotel. Buckle up please," he said distractedly.

Still not entirely convinced this man was actually my Uber driver I kept my hand on the inside handle the whole journey, though what I thought that would achieve I don't know. I was hardly going to open the door and commando roll out of a moving car, onto the hard cobblestones. He didn't make any small talk and I was glad. This obviously hadn't been his first rodeo transporting the perilously impaired, he must have known I would make no cognizant sense at all if asked any questions. At the hotel I left him idling on the side of the road, engrossed in his phone once more. Luckily there was no-one in the foyer and I made it up the narrow staircase with no issues, apart a few more bruises to add to the collection that I'd begun on my shins that morning. Once the hotel door was shut and locked I relieved my aching bladder, stripped and crawled into the freshly made bed. I was out before my head even hit the pillow.

**

The audience are beginning to fidget as they wait for me to escape the reveries of the past and begin. Those first memories of a holiday when everything was still normal and my biggest problems were a shamefully low tolerance for weed and a weak pelvic floor are painful. I was a different person, unblemished and untainted by the events yet to come. That person is so new and young and shiny looking compared to me now. I feel like I've aged a thousand years since then. If only I could reach back and grab that person, tell them to pack their bags and get back to the airport. Tell them to get out while the going was good. I cringe seeing her earnest face, thinking she was about to have a lovely break and then go back to her life, maybe a few pounds heavier, but basically unchanged. Shaking my head slightly, I try to banish the sour thoughts and get back to the planned lecture.

"Let's get started shall we?" I ask rhetorically, trying to sound as bright as possible, as though addressing a room full of primary school children.

I click the next slide into place – PACK

LIGHT/ESSENTIALS pops up on screen with a little clip-art picture of a suitcase I'd found. Scouring the ClipArt library for a suitable picture was a real blast from the past. It made me remember school IT lessons, creating presentations and absolutely needing the perfect Clip-art picture for every page. I really had to stop myself from breaking out the WordArt.

"If you are going to be away from your home, for any reason, then make sure you always pack light. If you are faced with an emergency situation don't bother trying to save your luggage, it will slow you down. Same as the safety announcement on an aeroplane; leave it. Your life is more important. My suggestion is to invest in a bumbag." A few groans drift out of the audience.

"I know what you're thinking, but we're a long way from the eighties shell-suit material bumbags of the past. Though honestly those super retro eighties bumbags are definitely coming back into style. I have two of them. There are plenty of good, sturdy models on the market since last year. Make sure to keep your essentials with you – passport or ID, phone, medication, torch and maybe even a small legal weapon. You don't need to be dying over a suitcase but having essentials with you might be the difference between life and death should something happen. Equally in your home make sure

you have a bugging out bag of critical items somewhere easily reachable with the same things included. Add in the imperatives like water, batteries and a first aid kit. There are plenty of guides online based on hurricane preparedness bags. Don't be caught out."

CHAPTER TWO: JONAH

I woke up in an unfamiliar bed, in an unfamiliar room but the crushing hangover that seemed to grip my entire body was an all too familiar feeling. Closing my eyes against the light I tried to remember where I was. The bed itself was too small and too empty, the room much too bright. I felt rancid, utterly rancid, with a headache that pulsed between my eyes at every heartbeat and a stomach that gurgled unpleasantly. From behind my clenched eyes I heard the meaty, wet fart of another person. It wasn't my girlfriend. Amelia would have been impressed by that effort but she didn't have a posterior large enough to create that kind of resonance. She also didn't have a diet bad enough to create that kind of smell. The stench hit me in the face like a manure covered shovel. I remembered where I was. The stag-do. Amsterdam. Turning away from the wave of smell, the springs screeched and lurched like a small craft being broken apart on a rough sea.

It was the second night I had spent away from my own bed and I missed it terribly. Homesickness washed over my clammy, hungover body. The night before last I'd slept in a hotel airport because Ross, the best man, had booked flights earlier than the trains had started to run and I didn't drive. I could have gotten a lift with some of the other guys but had decided to splash out on a room of my own. I'd told Amelia it was for convenience and so I could get a good night's sleep before the early morning flight. That was somewhat true but I desperately needed a day to myself to recharge my social battery before having to spend several days in continued company with no reprieve, especially if that company included Ross. He had been adamant the flights were so early because they were the cheapest available but as our relationship could be described as strained, if I were being polite, and I didn't trust that he hadn't booked them at that time just because he knew it would be inconvenient for me in particular. I needed some time to really feel my feelings all on my own, to harrumph and grump and huff and sigh about the injustice of it all. If I needed to I could have thrown myself on the floor like a toddler having a tantrum, beating the floor with my feet and fists without worrying about the impression I was giving off. I could mutter and chunter and swear without Amelia asking what I'd just said under my breath or rolling her eyes at me.

Amelia had a surprising amount of patience, but I was embarrassed at my often grouchy moods and more so that she'd become so used to them. Usually she left me alone to play video games and stew in my own childishness. It was the best thing for me really. It meant I had a chance to get over myself in my own time, rather than doubling down stubbornly like I was prone to do if pushed. It didn't stop her putting her arms around me when I got into bed at night or stop me from snuggling my face into the top of her hair, burrowing into her comforting smell and the metronome of her breath on my neck, her hand on my heart. I loved falling asleep with her like that, entwined together, until she got too hot and rolled away from me, mumbling into her pillow as she settled back into a deep sleep. We'd been together so long that she knew me completely. Once I sorted myself out, no words, explanation or apologies were needed. Our night-time embrace was the coming back to centre for me. It was my equilibrium. I usually made my best decisions in that calm place, in the drifting space between asleep and awake. The decision to attend this stag-do was not one of my best.

To dispel the ghost of her in the bed I sat up, narrowly avoiding giving myself a concussion on the bunk above. My headache threatened to spill my brains out onto the cheap polyester covers and I sucked at the fetid air, trying to dispel the pain. Standing up warily, wincing at my bare feet on a cold floor that didn't look all together clean, I held onto the bunk above until my vision stopped swimming. Gingerly I made my way to the shared bathroom, every footstep thudding through my entire body. Thankfully the water was hot and I resisted the urge to sit under the pelting stream with my head in my hands. Primarily because if I sat down I might not be able to get up again and secondly because I didn't think the gritty surface of the shower tray against my bare arse would help with the nausea of my hangover. It didn't take long for someone to knock on the door urgently, desperate for the toilet. I threw on my clothes in a rush, pulling my jeans up painfully as they stuck to my badly dried, still damp legs. My wet hair was already soaking the collar of my shirt. It made me think about my mother saying how wet hair would bring on a chill.

I opened the door testily to John, who could only grunt in greeting as he danced from foot to foot holding his crotch like a toddler. He dashed past me and I could hear a solid stream of urine hit the bowl before I'd even managed to close the door behind me. At least that was all he'd needed. I wasn't sure that not sure my delicate stomach could cope with any more close encounter odours. The walk back into the bedroom and the smell of many men huffing their fetid boozy breath into the enclosed dormitory was enough to enrage it. It smelt like a combination of old fish and chips and damp laundry.

Someone had pulled the curtain back across the

bright square of window and I could make out the rest of the stag-do members in varying states of consciousness and/or undress. Apart from John, who I could hear sighing in relief even through the door, was the stag; Stuart, Tommy, Tim, Keith and Ross. Apart from Ross we all knew each other well, having played five-a-side football every weekend since leaving school together. Ross was a new addition and, to me at least, not a very welcome one. When Tony had dropped out, saying his knees couldn't take the strain any more, we needed another member to be able to continue. Stuart had suggested someone he worked with who was interested. That was how I came to meet Ross. I didn't like him from the first moment I met him. Part of it was resentment at our tight knit group being intruded upon by someone new who didn't know our shared histories or our intrinsic conversational shorthand and part of it was because he was obviously a cocky twat. He took the game far more seriously than every other person there. We played to stay fit, stay in touch and maybe, although I'd be reluctant to admit it, to attempt to cling on to a little bit of our youth. Ross wanted to win and he had no qualms about using a slide tackle or a studs up hack at the ankles to get there. He tried to cover his competitiveness by claiming it was just a bit of fun, his hands up in the air if you dared to complain about aggressively being taken out on his quest for the ball. He was obviously having fun, that much was evident by his merriment when you fell or if you got hurt.

Ross laughed a lot but it wasn't an altogether pleasant sound. His taste in humour seemed only to be at the expense of others. He was the type of guy who cheered when a waitress dropped a tray of drinks, jubilant at someone else's embarrassment. As much as I was loathe to admit it that was preferable to when his focus rested on me. He seemed to have a special dislike for me, thinking me too liberal (we'd had a few run ins over politics), too soft (I assume because of the healthy communicative relationship with my girlfriend) and too worried about my appearance (hair gel). The last one was my particular bugbear, it wasn't vanity but in a life-long battle with self image. I was lean but if I wasn't careful lean would tip into skinny and before too long into downright emaciated. The rest of the guys knew about my struggles with food and exercise and didn't say anything about it. Ross on the other hand ferreted out weakness like a terrier with a rat. He'd shake it and shake it until its neck broke and you ended up losing your cool. That seemed to bring him the most joy, he'd grin a smile replete with teeth and store that weakness away for future reference, so he could bring it out again when you least expected, pushing and probing at the sore spot like a tongue exploring a loose tooth.

I'd debated leaving the team all together but I didn't want Ross to chase me away from my friends and I also needed a team sport to stop myself taking exercise too far. I'd tried the gym but it was easy for me to become obsessive, spending hours there on my own, earbuds in, testing myself against my own personal bests. How many reps did I do yesterday? Could I beat them? Could I turn the treadmill up just a little bit higher? Were the scales showing a number a little bit lower? Once I started getting fixated on the gym it wasn't long before the calorie counting started and I ended up on a diet of meal replacement shakes and not a lot else. Football let me exercise without anxiety creeping into the corners, allowing it to be fun and not excessive. Ever since Ross had joined the team, the joy of it had been coloured somewhat by my annoyance at him but I didn't want to give it up. Instead I stayed and gritted my teeth and now I was in Amsterdam, my gritted smile creaking under the strain of not disappointing Stuart.

Rubbing my jaw I made my way out onto the landing. Tommy was standing at the top, swaying gently but alarmingly.

"Alright mate?" I said, gently putting my hand on his shoulder so as not to catapult him down the steep staircase.

"Just gearing myself up Joe," he muttered, keeping his eyes on the steps.

"Come on. Let's get some fresh air," I said, eyeing the stairs with trepidation myself.

We made our way out into the cool mid-morning air but the smell of damp laundry followed us. I sniffed at Tommy experimentally and more obviously than intended. He turned to me sheepishly.

"Yeah I know. I had to do a load of washing the night before we left, and it didn't dry properly before I packed it. I thought it would dry out in the suitcase."

My mouth flapped uselessly, not knowing where to begin but before I could formulate a response, Ross barrelled out of the doorway between us. I was jealous of his vigour. I was still fighting the urge to lay on the floor and moan like a Victorian ghost. Apart from glazed and slightly bloodshot eyes he looked no worse for wear. How he managed it was a minor miracle considering the amount he'd put away since the beginning of yesterday morning. He slung his arm around both my and Tommy's necks, bringing our heads together with a jerk. It was obvious that he hadn't made use of the hostel's facilities. He smelt of old booze and unwashed armpits. I struggled against his grasp. Being so close to the assaulting smells of both Tommy and Ross combined was going to make me boak.

"Oi oi lads," Ross shouted into the quiet morning street. "What's the plan then?" he asked, seemingly having forgotten that he was the best man and thus trip organiser. "Big fat spliff and a fry up is it?"

The thought of that, the combined smells of both men, and my all encompassing hangover finally won over. I stumbled over to the edge of the canal to vomit messily into the water below. I was mortified. I didn't want to be one of those tourists, randomly expelling their bodily functions in the street, but I simply had no control over my stomach. It clenched and emptied of its own accord, over and over again, splashing its contents noisily into the murk below.

I heard the cheers from the men behind me at my sordid exhibition but I could only rest my clammy forehead weakly against the railing while I composed myself. When my stomach had recalibrated somewhat, I managed to shrug off the small backpack I'd brought with me. Rummaging around, I brought out a bottle of water and a packet of paracetamol. I sipped at the water, hoping my stomach wouldn't rebel. I threw back two paracetamol and chased it with a gulp from the bottle. My stomach burbled angrily at the caustic pills. Next came a gurgle from a miniature mouthwash bottle I'd bought at the airport the day before. I spat out the burning liquid, and the little chunks that remained in my mouth, and turned to face the group. I felt a lot better physically but I was embarrassed. I made my way back over to them, the cold air burning the insides of my minty mouth.

"Hahaha check out the boy scout!" yelled Ross, "Always prepared eh Pretty Boy?" He laughed, slapping me painfully on the back.

I wished there was enough left in my stomach to vomit on his shoes. I was already pretty tired of the laddish banter, but with a strain, I smiled back at Ross, resisting the urge to make faces as he turned his back. I wanted to stick out my tongue at the back of his head, like I used to do to my brother when we were kids.

**

I can't bring myself to talk about what really happened in Amsterdam with Amelia. I wish it was because of a 'what goes on tour stays on tour' kind of pact I'd made with other members of the stag do but it's not. I can't talk to her about it because I can not bear to see her face when I tell her what I've seen and done or what happened to the people who had been in our flat for dinner, out for drinks or sat next to us at weddings. She doesn't push me to talk but she does go on the internet and seemingly devour every scrap of information she can get her hands on the events of Amsterdam last year. I often go to sleep bathed in the glow from her iPad as she scrolls some forum or news site looking for information. She wears headphones so I can't hear any of the videos that she finds. I can't stand the thought of hearing it out loud in our warm and cosy flat. She found a plethora of forums and survivors' groups for those dealing with trauma but I'm not interested. I don't want to discuss the minutiae with a bunch of strangers, especially if I can't even do it with the person I love most in the world.

I haven't asked her but I think she's doing this to understand me better, the new me at least. Our relationship had been so good before I left. We understood each other in that way that makes other people a bit queasy. Now I was damaged in a way she didn't understand because she hadn't been through what I had. I know she keeps in touch with some of the other guys' partners. I know it because of the gentle way she sometimes put things to me, like they had discussed it at length to practice or smooth out a certain tactic or modus operandi.

I knew she put it to them first because when she sat me down and showed me a booking page for Jennifer's talk she presented the iPad to me carefully, like something that might bite if I moved too fast. At the sight of Jennifer's face I can feel the sting of its teeth anyway. She looks completely different to when we met in Amsterdam but I'd recognise her anywhere. I read the details of the speech she is going to give and surprise both of us by clicking 'Book Now'. I don't know if its a good decision or not. I don't trust my decisions any more.

CHAPTER THREE: JENNIFER

I drifted into a fitful doze, seeming only to skim the surface between wakefulness and sleep; accosted by a plethora of bright, vivid dreams. It was the kind of sleep you have in the midst of a fever, that makes you worry about the hold you have on your sanity. Finally, past the kaleidoscope of colours and Dalí-esque images came a very promising dream about Evan from the accounts department in the break room with no shirt on. Without a word he took me forcefully in his muscled grasp and traced his lips down my neck. I shuddered at his touch. He looked me in the eyes and I knew that he wanted to kiss me, like I wanted to kiss him. His face came towards mine, his soft lips parting slightly. Instead of a satisfied sigh or sweet nothings slipping between those pink, perfect lips, Evan began to shriek. Not a human shriek, but a pulsing and rhythmic electronic noise that no human would be capable of making. His ice blue eyes were full of panic as his mouth continued its mechanical keening.

I jumped awake. The sound was still in the room, reverberating against the insides of my skull. It took me longer than it should have done to realise the sound was coming from my phone on the night stand. It was a tone I'd never heard it make before. I batted at it, like an angry cat, from my face down position on the pillow, willing it to stop its infernal racket but only succeeding in knocking it under the bed to caterwaul incessantly amongst the dust bunnies.

Crawling out of the warm, comfy bed to rescue it, I stretched to my full length on the chilly floor to tease it out with my fingertips. I looked at the screen: **'EMERGENCY ALERT – EXTERNAL THREAT TO LIFE. SEEK SHELTER. AWAIT FURTHER INSTRUCTIONS'** the text message screamed out at me from the lock screen. Fumbling with the passcode I finally managed to click the message with trembling fingers. There was no further information than just those eleven words.

The only times I'd heard of an emergency alert were either in a Hollywood disaster movie or that one time on the news when all the inhabitants of Hawaii had been told there was a ballistic missile threat and to seek shelter. I hoped this would be the same kind of miscommunication. I hoped that somewhere deep in the bowels of some government facility was an intern who had pressed the wrong button and was currently sweating bullets. Surely there would be another message along shortly explaining the error; "Phew, sorry about that folks! False alarm!" Any minute. Maybe it had been a good idea to pack all of that extra underwear after all.

I kept staring at the screen, willing the retraction to arrive and reading the original message over and over, hoping to glean some further meaning from the small paragraph. It was ominously vague and my imagination began to run away with itself; What was the threat to life? What were we seeking shelter from? When would instructions arrive? I stared at the phone for ten, fifteen, twenty minutes. No error message arrived. No further instructions were incoming. Shit.

Pulling on the rumpled clothes I'd discarded for my nap I ventured down the vertigo inducing stairs to the foyer. I wanted to see if there was anyone around to ask about the creepy message but also if there was somewhere I could buy a very cold can of something fizzy for my desiccated mouth. It stuck together at every pained swallow and tasted like I'd licked the bottom of an ashtray. Hopefully the nice clerk would be behind the desk and would tell me in soothing, dulcet tones that everyone had been previously briefed about the emergency alert drill, that I wouldn't have known as I'd only flown in this morning. He would laugh good naturedly at my concern, tell me everything would be fine and ask if I wanted a dinner reservation made for me. I'd thank him, tut at my own unwarranted panic and think about what a good anecdote it would make to highlight the perils of weed induced paranoia the next time I was at the pub with my mates. I crossed my fingers behind my back as I descended.

There was no-one behind the desk and the front door of the hotel was wide open, letting in cold air, birdsong and nothing else. There was not a soul on the street outside, no pedestrians, no cars, no bikes – no-one at all. Walking over to the desk I peered around the back of it, hoping to see the clerk hanging up keys, restocking brochures or something equally mundane. Instead there was a note left on the top of the desk, hastily scrawled in English; "Gone to be with my family. Good luck." Double shit. So it definitely wasn't a planned event with nothing to worry about. The only person I'd spoken to in this country apart from two Uber drivers and a server in a cafe had abandoned his post to hunker down with his own family. Brilliant. Absolutely fucking marvellous. The front door standing wide open to the desolate street was starting to freak me out. I hurried over and closed it, shuddering at the thought of what it was being closed against; nuclear missiles, radioactive spiders, werewolves, who bloody knew! I snicked across the locks on the inside of the door and made my way back up the dizzyingly twisted staircase to my room, my thirst unsatiated but temporarily forgotten.

Sitting on the bed in my room I tried to access the internet on my phone. No Service. I tried waving the handset around near the window, in the bathroom and even ventured out into the corridor to wave it around some more but it resolutely told me – No Service. There were two options; sit inside hoping it was nothing and maybe waste a whole day of my holiday peering out of my window like a paranoid freak. Or, attempt to go out and get more information and hope I wasn't eaten by a rampaging stampede of rhinoceros loose from the local zoo or whatever else the message was warning against. My stomach rumbled and that settled the matter.

I ventured back downstairs. The street was still empty and eerily quiet. It was giving me the heebie-jeebies. I'd noted on my arrival the ingenuity of countless people all riding their bikes across and down narrow side streets without hitting one another or any pedestrians, but now there was no-one. Not one person. I wondered if a nuclear apocalypse had occurred while I'd had my white-out nap. What if I was now the only woman left alive in the world? I didn't much fancy my chances having to make fire with twigs and flint, having to catch food and not die from appendicitis or an infected graze. I'd never even been camping before as I didn't like the thought of a Portaloo or squatting in the woods.

There was a bike rack outside the hotel with a few bicycles awaiting their owners' return. They reminded me of horses, in the old Westerns my dad used to watch, patiently tied up outside the saloon. I decided to take one. I'd booked a bike as part of my hotel package so surely it wasn't really stealing. Also, I thought, it would probably be easier to traverse the nuclear wasteland I was about to enter if I could do it quickly. Maybe later I could use it to barter with other survivors, if there were any, in the new post apocalyptic dog-eat-dog society.

The saying "as easy as riding a bike" is a big fat lie. It's not easy to ride a bike if the only forms of transport you have used in the last decade are the tube or the night bus. The seat was too high and I could find no way to lower it. I balanced on my tippy-toes feeling very unsafe. There was no helmet and the large body of water next to the hotel had no guard rail to stop me careening straight into it. I put one foot on the pedal, holding myself steady with only two toes on the floor. Two toes on a foot that badly needed a pedicure. I wondered what I would have to barter in the new world for a pedicure. It didn't bear thinking about.

My balance on two feet was not the best and, with only two toes on the ground, the metal contraption was swaying alarmingly. It didn't feel safe. Taking a deep breath and holding it, I pushed off from the ground. By some small miracle my right foot found the other pedal and I was away. For a moment euphoria swept though me. It quickly dissipated as I rattled my way down the street, the jostling of the thin metal bike on the uneven surface sending reverberations through every one of my bones. It was making the little paunch that I'd been determined to get rid of for the last six to ten years wobble dramatically like a cake on a tumble dryer. I'm sure my fearful rictus grin and wildly dancing body fat would not have been a sexy look, but luckily the street was still deserted so no one could see my jibbly, wibbly, wobbly shame.

I cycled along the pavement, jerkily twisting the handlebars from side to side to keep my balance, breathless from panic and exertion. Stealing glances sideways as I went, the city didn't look like a nuclear wasteland; birds were still singing and trees were still dancing in the breeze. The sky wasn't scorched and full of the ash-like snow of nuclear fallout. I passed the coffee-shop I'd been in earlier, closed and dark within. Finally, I started to see people, all making their way down to a source of increasing noise. I was relieved. There was obviously an impromptu concert or some top notch street entertainment that had attracted everyone to one place. As I got closer I realised the sound was a low level murmuring, punctuated with exclamations of shock. It was the type of sound that I'd been, so far, lucky enough to only hear on the news - the surprised and terrified awe of lots of people simultaneously witnessing something terrible.

Bumbling up behind the crowd I dismounted ungraciously, resisting the urge to rub the feeling back into my arse cheeks in case passers-by thought I was some kind of pervert. I left the bike leaning against one of the black railings overlooking the canal. The crowd was huge already, sprawling out from the canal's lip like a trailing limb. People were packed in tight and jostling one another. Everyone seemed desperate to get a look at what was in the water below. I could smell the sweet tang of a couple of joints in the crowd and the sugary scent of something fried, like doughnuts. My mouth watered. I was starving.

From my vantage point I couldn't see what the crowd had gathered around. I was far too short. I bopped around in the back, trying to sneak a peak over shoulders and through the holes of arms on hips. I slid into gaps as soon as someone moved, having had plenty of practice of this kind of crowd Jenga whenever I'd wanted to get to the front at a gig. It didn't even smell that different from the last concert I'd been to; sweat, cigarettes and weed. Eventually I decided to drop my English sensibilities and do a bit of shoving to get to the front of the crowd. Not many people noticed. They were too focused on what was in front of them. Either that, or they were too European to care. The air was electrically charged and there was a buzz of anticipation from the crowd. Those standing on the bridge over the canal all seemed to have their phones out, trained on the canal below. They were pointing and babbling excitedly to their neighbours in Dutch. I had no idea what they were saying.

Finally, I managed to get near enough to the edge of the canal to be able to see what all of the hubbub was about. My brain, still pretty addled from too much THC, couldn't process what it was seeing. It was too weird to fathom. I wondered if I had wandered onto a movie filming on location, and soon a pissed-off director was going to yank me out of the crowd and berate me in rapid-fire Dutch for ruining his scene. This couldn't really be happening. Could it?

**

'INVEST IN A SATELLITE PHONE' says the next slide in a rather jaunty font that had taken me far too long to choose. Next to it was another piece of clip-art that had taken me nearly as long to select as the jaunty font. I'm a little embarrassed at my crude effort but it's too late to do anything about

it now so I continue.

"Yes I know they are expensive but if you are going to be somewhere you don't know very well they could literally be a life saver. You don't ever want to be in an information black spot or somewhere that you can not easily tell someone where you are. If it's a black spot for you then it is a black spot for rescuers as well. No one is saying ditch the iPhone, but don't solely rely on it. If enough people are trying to call all at once then the lines will effectively be down and you will be on your own. Take it from me that is not a nice feeling."

I try to smile at the audience with a 'you know what I mean' shake of the head but it feels false on my face, a grotesque mask of false joviality. That 'No Service' alert on my phone was a portent for the end. I was totally alone in a country I'd never been to before and didn't know the language of. I didn't realise the network was already swamped with calls and had been since I'd been smoking myself into oblivion. I had mistakenly and perhaps arrogantly thought physical maps were a relic of the past and I'd planned on just using the map on my phone when sight-seeing. Now I have a mid-range waterproof satellite phone with GPS tracking and downloadable maps. I never want to feel the same way I did standing in that hotel, totally alone and vulnerable, ever again.

If only that had been the worst of it. If only I'd been alone in that hotel and stayed put, gone back up to my room and not made my way down to the crowd. As I remember standing next to that canal, the cold wind drying the sweat on my back, looking down the sheer edges below, my stomach cramps painfully. I walk back to the low table and take a long gulp of water. It's going nowhere. It sits resolutely at the top of my stomach, making me sloshy, threatening to make a reappearance. I burp quietly into the back of my hand. It tastes of acid and regret.

"TIME TO LEARN SOME NEW SKILLS" the next slide announces. This is starting to be less like a talk on my experience and more like a school assembly by the technologically challenged careers advisor. I look out into the audience and see a few bored faces already.

"How many of you know how to ride a bike?" I ask them. A few hands go up tentatively, looking around to see if they are the only ones.

"Put your hands down if it's been more than a year since you last rode a bike," The majority of the hands go down again.

"Yup, that's what I thought. I thought I knew how to ride a bike, until I got to Amsterdam. Oh it'll be easy, I thought. They don't say it's just like riding a bike for nothing right?" I ignore the polite snickers from the audience. "It's not just like riding a bike. I don't know about you guys but I am significantly heavier than when I was a kid and my centre of gravity is very different. The reason I bring up bikes is that it's relatively cheap and easy to learn to ride a bike. You can pick up an inexpensive bike online and spend a couple of hours falling over in the park until you get it right. Learning to drive a car takes longer, costs more and is less reliable. What if there is not a car available? What if it runs out of petrol or breaks down? A bike isn't going to give you those issues and it's faster than running when you need to get away. It also covers much more ground than being on foot." There is the ghost of someone saying those very words in my ear.

It feels as though I'm effectively talking to myself or, worse, lecturing those in the audience. This isn't what I wanted. I'm not a scholar or an expert. I'm just some woman who got incredibly lucky; lucky enough that I am able to tell people what happened and see if they can put those experiences to some use, should they need to.

"Okay, real talk guys. This wasn't meant to be

some kind of boring school lecture. I'm not an expert and I'm not here to preach at you. I'm just fortunate enough to still have a voice to tell you what happened. I didn't do anything fancy. All I did was survive and I made an awful lot of mistakes along the way. Let's ditch this projector crap." I turn off the projector and turn to the audience. "I'll tell you what happened out there, and you just yell out if you have any questions. Sound good?" There is some murmuring, which I take as assent.

Hitching up the trousers of my suit, I sit cross legged on the floor of the stage, the same way I would on my sofa, and close my eyes. I have tried for many months to banish the visceral, technicolour images of my ill-fated holiday. Now I let them come, and start to speak into the microphone.

CHAPTER FOUR: JONAH

Ross had been the one to insist that we go to the pub after every match, straight from the pitch. As a group we'd often go out on a Saturday night but I liked being able to go home and soak in a hot bath and get dressed into something smart before heading out. Ross on the other hand, was desperate to start drinking as soon as possible, he was often hinting at it way before the rest of us were ready to finish the game. His surly muttering in the background about wasting valuable drinking time got on my nerves. Why did he even bother to play if his only weekend concern was being in the pub? Sitting in the pub with sweat rapidly cooling on my back and rising into the air like morning mist made me very conscious about the way I smelt. Every little movement tumbled flakes of dried mud from my kit like a trail of breadcrumbs when I went to the bar. It left me awkward, self conscious and off balance, exactly how Ross liked people to feel.

It wasn't a proper pitch, just a marked off section in the local park. There were some public toilets and an outside tap that was unrelentingly freezing, even in the middle of summer but nowhere to have a proper shower. Not that the thought of entering a shower block with someone like Ross filled me with anything other than all encompassing dread. He'd be the kind of person to flick your bare arse with a knotted towel or to say something disparaging about the size of your knob in front of all the other guys while dancing around shoving his in your face, like a chimp showing off. It's what he reminded me of; a chimp with a leering, toothy grin and the ability to rip your face off just for the hell of it.

It was at one of those post match drinks, when I was absently picking the flaking mud off my arm like peeling sunburn, that Stuart announced he had asked his long standing, and long suffering, girlfriend to marry him. His eyes were shining brightly as he accepted pats on the back and heartfelt congratulations. A few of us looked at each other with consternation - it was inevitable our own girlfriends were going to hear about the engagement. I loved Amelia and had been thinking about popping the question for some time but was ashamed to admit that a big project at work had stolen the majority of my recent focus. I hadn't the energy or the capacity after a long day at work to sneakily steal one of her rings for sizing and then stare at hundreds of seemingly similar looking rings in a jeweller, racked with anxiety about whether or not I was picking the correct one. After deciding on the piece of jewellery I thought she would be happy to wear for (hopefully!) the rest of her life I would then have to think of a way to ask her that seemed like a big enough gesture. Flash mob wedding engagements on social media had really ruined it for the rest of us. There was nothing wrong with a candlelit dinner in a tasteful restaurant and going down on one knee after dessert. It was a classic for a reason. I didn't want to have to learn dance moves and lip sync.

Stuart's fiancee Cheryl was a mousy looking girl with a savage sense of humour and a staggeringly dirty laugh. She also had the ability to consume alcohol at a rate that put the majority of us to shame. I knew she would probably involve Amelia in some capacity in the wedding and I'd have to see her looking longingly at Cheryl's wedding dress and quirky table decorations sometime in the near future. The thought of the look on her face at yet another wedding that wasn't ours almost broke my heart. I could either endure that or pull my finger out and buy a ring to surprise her with after the wedding. It might make me look like I was copying Stuart but if I did it beforehand it would look like I was trying to steal Stuart and Cheryl's thunder. Yet more impossible choices to make. I don't know why we are so desperate to become adults when we're kids - apart from a few limited perks, most of the time the constant decision making means being an adult is the absolute worst. Even as I congratulated Stuart the thoughts of Amelia and her reaction began to dampen my mood.

As Stuart's oldest and, I believed, closest friend I had taken it for granted that the role of best man would fall to me. It had seemed a foregone conclusion in my mind. As I'd never planned a stag do before and I wanted to be prepared. The next few days were spent either daydreaming about or googling some tentative plans – a countryside B&B, a pub crawl along the blustery seafront culminating in fish and chips or an adventure weekend with archery and axe throwing. I'd even started a list of places that looked nice, that I was hoping to share with Stuart in the pub after next week's game. I had fantasies of Stuart bringing it up as part of his wedding speech, announcing what a triumph it had been and toasting my success. Or how it would be brought up in years to come, the guys looking wistful and waxing lyrical about what fun we'd had, and the memories we made on that golden weekend. It was a stupid, prideful presumption which certainly came before a very big fall.

I failed multiple times to get Stuart on his own in the pub after the next week's game. I was so excited to tell him about the ideas and places and plans that I was almost bouncing in my chair. But I couldn't seem to quite catch him alone, he was either deep in conversation with someone else or on his way to the bar or the toilet. After watching and waiting, I jumped into Keith's seat when he went to get the next round in, placing myself finally next to Stuart. I had just opened my mouth when Ross turned in his seat, slinging his arm around Stuart's shoulder. Loudly, and with more than a little slurring, he announced he was going to be Stu's best man and that the stag do was going to be epic. Stuart looked at me sheepishly and shrugged. Realisation dawned on why I hadn't been able to get him on his own all night. He'd been trying to avoid this conversation and leave it up to Ross to break the news. Disappointment lodged in my throat and I tried to wash it away with a large gulp of beer, trying to give myself enough time to rearrange my face. Striving for happiness I'd only managed a mixture of hurt, annoyance and fake bonhomie. Not only were my feelings bruised at Ross being given the title of best man over me, but I was also coming to realise that a stag do organised by him was not going to be low-key and pleasant. It was going to be utter carnage.

I didn't want to be in one of those stag do groups that went somewhere culturally interesting and acted like a big group of drunken louts. However, I suspected that was exactly what Ross had in mind. The group grew excited, throwing around suggestions; Benidorm, Prague, Budapest, Vegas, Brighton and so on. I thought of the beautiful architecture of Prague or Budapest and having to walk around it blitzed, and probably wearing something with a massive todger on it. My grin was beginning to cave in on itself, mutating swiftly into a cringing grimace. I wondered if there was a way to get out of it. Could I buy some plaster of Paris and pretend I'd broken my ankle? Maybe I could ask Amelia to text the group to inform them that I was currently missing after a suspicious boating accident? That seemed maybe a step too far. But telling him I didn't want to go on his stag do made me feel I would be disappointing Stuart, a man I'd known and considered my closest friend for decades, just because I didn't like his vicious little mate and his predictable, pedestrian plans.

The boys debated the various booze and boob advantages of each location. There was even talk of a spreadsheet.

"I can't believe I didn't think of it before!" Ross roared over the conversation and laughter, slapping his forehead in a comical show. "How did we not think of......Amsterdam?!" he yelled, arms in the air like Oprah telling a whole studio audience they were about to get a free car. This crowd, quite like that audience, went crazy. I didn't join in with the cheering and whooping. The grin was slipping sideways off my face at an alarming rate.

"What's wrong Joe-Joe?" Ross shouted

deafeningly across the table, seeing the look on my face.

"Will the old ball and chain not let you go on a boy's weekend eh? Eh?" he wheedled.

It was a classic example of Ross finding a weak spot and mashing all the buttons until he found the one that would make me lose my rag. I'd fallen for it countless times before only to be met with his raised hands, eyes wide in fake innocence and protestations along the lines of - "ooh touchy, it was just a joke Joe-Joe," or "hit a nerve have I Joe-Joe?" or "just a bit of banter Joe-Joe, no need to take it so seriously," all the while looking at me with his sharp weasel grin, willing me to make a show of myself in front of the other guys. He needed to prove that he was the fun one and I was the killjoy, party-pooper. I had to try my hardest not to say anything, not to let my temper get the better of me.

"Not at all," I said, as calmly as I could, taking a deep draught of my drink and wondering what Amelia would say when I told her. I doubted she'd be thrilled about the idea. Like me.

Stuart took me aside as I was putting my coat on to leave.

"Look mate, I didn't ask you because..." I cut

him off with a raised hand.

"It's OK. You don't have to justify yourself to me Stu. I'm not your mum, you can do what you like."

"You're alright about it?" he asked, stooping slightly, to look me full in the face.

"Yup," I said, before drinking the last mouthful of beer in my glass and zipping up my coat, hoping it would be enough to stop the conversation in its tracks. I had the prickling sense of jealousy sloshing around with the lager in my belly and felt even more guilty as I saw how my answer had lit up his face.

"Good. I'm really glad Jona..." I coughed to stop him. My eyes flicking towards the rest of the group, hoping they hadn't heard him. The last thing I needed was Ross getting this newest, sorest morsel between his teeth.

"Joe," Stuart finished, shaking his head at my protestations over the use of my full name. "I'm really glad Joe. I think it's going to be a right laugh," He clapped me on the shoulder. "You'll see."

I wish he'd been right. I really really do.

*****

The phrase "What if" is my new, almost constant, companion. It looms large in my head, neon letters blazing. It is there from the time I get up to the time I go to bed. What if I had insisted we go somewhere else? What if I had convinced Stuart of a different plan? What if I'd decided not to go at all? Maybe that plaster of Paris idea hadn't been so crazy at all. What if? What if? What if? It goes round and around my head like a song that you can't stop humming. A poisonous earworm.

I run the scenarios over and over, like a football coach debating various tactics. I run through them in the twilight between sleep and wakefulness, out loud and in my head. I batter and bruise myself with the choices that I took. But it all comes down to luck. I was unlucky to be in Amsterdam when I was, but I was lucky I made it out. Not all of Stu's Stags enjoyed the same luck. But in my darkest hours, when I'm tired of running every single decision through my head, when I'm at my lowest and the guilt is an almost tangible weight on my chest, I almost wish I was one of the ones who didn't make it out. At least their suffering is over. Mine feels never-ending.

CHAPTER FIVE: JENNIFER

Making my way to the edge of the canal, I looked down into the water. The stone walls of the canal's basin were high and almost vertical, falling away beneath my feet to a roiling and broiling murk below. The water was full of creatures. Creatures that clawed and threw themselves at the sheer walls, desperately trying to get to the people above them. Desperate to get to me. They clamoured at the sides, surging against one another in their determination to escape. I was staggered by their number and utterly confused as to why they were there.

Like a grotesque Jacob's Ladder they pulled themselves up each other's bodies before tumbling back into the water below. The creatures who must have fallen in first were at the bottom of the pile of seething bodies, many of them apparently drowned, having been trampled and submerged by their cohorts who had used their bodies to frantically try propelling themselves up the sides of the canal's basin. Some had started to bloat already, a few were beginning to float away from the melee, swept away by the flow of the water. The crowd was standing perilously close, me included, straining to see over the sides. It reminded me of dropping bread into the water on a family holiday to Cape Cod as a kid, watching the slick, furious bodies of huge fish knocking each other out of the way to get to the soggy morsels. These creatures had the same feral, desperate stare as the fish I'd fed all those years ago.

The creatures weren't making any sounds that could be discerned as human, no words or phrases, but a mixture of grunting and keening. Those sounds mixed with the splashing of their frenzied attempts to escape were so loud that it made me want to put my hands over my ears. It was obvious to the crowd of us standing at the canal's edge that, despite current appearances, these creatures had once been human themselves. They were all wearing clothes, jeans and shirts and dresses, some more torn than others. I spotted one with a camera slung around their neck, its lens cracked and pouring water. Another still held on tightly to a selfie stick, bashing it uselessly against the stone wall, a pair of sunglasses held on by only one ear, the other side a riot of torn flesh.

They may have once been human, but their faces now were anything but. Their eyes rolled in a bovine way, unable to focus. Their mouths were mashing maws, teeth and gums and yawning darkness, gnashing open and closed, tongues bloated and raw looking, like something you'd see in a butcher's window. Many were missing huge patches of skin, but the flesh underneath didn't bleed and the wounds looked too deep to have been sustained by merely falling into a canal. I could see the deep yellow hue of fat peeking through ravaged skin and, on more than one, the quick flash of white bone nestled deep within. None of this seemed to be slowing them down. I watched one woman try to grip onto the wall with a hand that was no longer there. The stump slid down the stone, bringing all the vegetation with it, to rain gently onto her face. It was hypnotic in its repugnance.

I was broken out of my reverie by someone knocking into my back, sending me close to the edge. The toe of my shoe peeked out into the air. It drove the creatures into more of a frenzy, reaching up towards me. I lurched back with a sound that was a cross between a sob and a yell. A silly noise, full of terror. I'm not too proud to admit it. I made many, much worse noises during the rest of my time in Amsterdam. Pushing back against the crowd, I hoped to slip through a gap and back to relative safety, not wanting one of those things to get hold of me and drag me down into the thrashing morass with them. Unsurprisingly most of the crowd were recording with their phones, rather than paying any real attention. They didn't seem to realise they weren't at a concert, taking shaky footage they would never watch again, but instead were in very real, very immediate danger. Have you ever seen those viral videos of tourists standing around blithely while an elephant charges or a hippo rises from the depths? That's what these people reminded me of. They didn't pay me any attention either but shifted and moved enough for me to get some distance between myself and the lip of the canal. The crowd had gathered in size, even since I'd been there. It was densely packed with people hoping to get a peep. They were all too happy to fill into the gap that I had just vacated.

I managed to get into the halfway point of the throng when the first scream tore through the crowd.

**

I don't know exactly what happened. There are plenty of videos online from the people who were recording it. They get taken down pretty quickly but another one always pops up in its place. Grief voyeurs always want to get their kicks by watching someone else's tragedy, while safe and sound on their sofas at home. I don't need to watch it. I wake up too many nights with the ghost of that scream ringing in my ears. For me, that first scream was a klaxon, and hearing it again on a phone or computer might permanently shatter the ice-thin surface of my mental health for good.

When I first returned from Amsterdam, social media was awash with videos and articles and posts and tweets and memes about what had happened. Everyone had an opinion and the conspiracy theorists were out in force. One of the wildest theories I heard was that it was all the fault of bees. Yup you heard me right, the little fuzzy insects we were always told that were on the brink of extinction and without whom the ecosystem would collapse. Bees. There's a tiny faction of people who think that bees carry the infection that will make you into one of those creatures. The more militant believers actually dress up in black and yellow outfits and smoke bees out of their hives so they can exterminate them. They call themselves The Smokers, which always struck me as a pretty feeble name. However, they've been so prolific it's now a criminal offence to wantonly kill bees. It comes with a pretty hefty prison sentence.

They might be odd but they're perhaps not as crazy as those who think it is the fault of birds. The same kind of concept, birds picking up infection and flying it across the world. There have been several small outbreaks since Amsterdam, and these people are always quick to tell you that there were birds present before the creatures appeared. It's futile to even attempt explaining to them that there are birds pretty much everywhere in the world. I once saw a *video of one of those people literally screaming at pre-packaged chicken in the supermarket. After seeing that, I logged off and haven't logged back on since. I don't want to see a Buzzfeed article with some randomer's opinions on what caused the outbreak, and the poisonous comment section below from people who weren't there and don't understand.*

A hand goes up in the audience. I nod at them. They are reasonably far away but I can still tell that their face is not a happy one. He gestures tersely for the microphone that the sound technician is carrying up to his seat.

"If you're not an expert, then why are you here?" he asks gruffly. It sets off a low murmuring. Some in agreement and some at the audacity of the question. A few people are shooting him accusatory looks. I stare back at him, not answering. My unwavering gaze unnerves him and he gives the microphone back to the embarrassed sound technician who takes it and jogs back towards the stage. His eyes are wide at the awkward silence.

I'm pretty pissed off at the question. More so because he's kind of got a point. I don't really know why I'm doing this. I thought it was something close to altruism, trying to give some insight to others in case they ever found themselves in a similar situation. But it's starting to feel like a very public kind of therapy. The organisers told me that they had reached out to a few people to speak, but with no success. I'm starting to realise why. It's bringing up all kinds of memories and feelings that I'm not sure I wanted to remember or experience again. But I'm here now and there is only another hour to get through before I can grab my bag, get myself home to my duvet and a half finished bottle of Pinot waiting for me on the coffee table.

"I had hoped that hearing what it was really like from someone like me - not a scholar, not a journalist but just some unlucky pleb who found themselves in the middle of it - could potentially help some other hapless soul who finds themselves in a similar situation. But, there are plenty of field guides you can read. Or magazine articles. Perhaps you would prefer one of the many medical studies available. You are welcome to peruse any of them, if you don't want to listen to me. There's the door." I gesture at the well lit exit sign. The man coughs nervously, and shifts uncomfortably in his seat but doesn't leave.

I used to be so worried about being nice, so concerned about being rude and or sounding aggressive. Now I couldn't give a shit. Since Amsterdam, and my semi-retreat from society, I seem to have lost that filter. I'm not entirely sure if that's a good or a bad thing.

CHAPTER SIX: JONAH

I didn't help with the organising of the stag do. Part of it was churlishness at not being chosen as the best man, probably a bigger part than I'd like to admit, but the rest was not wanting to have to spend any more time with Ross than was absolutely necessary. If he wanted all of the responsibility then he could have it. I thought of it less as petulance and more of preserving some semblance of my sanity and temper. My face had an uncanny ability to broadcast exactly how I felt across my features, it was something I'd never really gotten a handle on. The thought of having to work hard to look happy about plans for live sex shows or brothels was not appealing. Neither was the anticipation of having to fake laugh at the planning of pranks for my normally reserved and sensitive friend. The thought of him stripped naked and tied to a lamppost or lustily stuffing notes into the G-string of a stripper made my whole body cringe. I'd never been laddish and I had no intention of starting now.

Stupidly I'd purchased a tour guide for Amsterdam once it was confirmed that was the destination but before I'd known that I would not actually be the best man. Irregardless, I'd read it on breaks at work or after Amelia had gone to bed. It had seemed harsh to be pouring through a guide book for a holiday in front of someone who was not invited. Almost like scoffing cake in front of someone on a diet. I wished I hadn't bought it but I couldn't stop looking at it. I was like a teenager with their first dirty magazine. The process of reading it felt furtive and clandestine but it was also almost physically painful to do so. There was so much culture on offer, so many museums and galleries and that was only on the first page. I realised with horror that it wasn't Amelia, it was actually me on the diet and instead of a good meal of culture and experience I was going to have to endeavour to satiate my appetite with a fast-food diet of weed, cheap lager and live sex shows.

Ross set up a WhatsApp group almost immediately and included all of the members of the stag do. Anxiety settled in my chest at every ping of notification from the fast moving group of messages. I thought about muting the group but that made me more anxious, I couldn't bear the thought of missing out on some important information even if the majority of the messages so far had just been lascivious ponderings or a slew of memes. I tried contributing some vanilla suggestions; cocktail tasting or a Segway tour of the city to no avail. The yawning silence after each suggestion was more than enough to show me that my ideas were not welcome and would most definitely, unequivocally, not be happening. So I answered the questions that needed to be answered and paid my share of the money that needed to be paid, and kept my mouth shut on any further proposals.

Paying my share of flights and accommodation into Ross's bank account, I was sorely tempted to put something like "crack funds" or "gigolo payments" instead I settled on my initials. This stag do was really bringing out the worst parts of my personality. It was making me uncomfortable and grumpy, swinging wildly between blaming myself and blaming Ross, with no respite. From the little I'd seen of his plan, when I steeled myself to be able to trawl the WhatsApp chat, the trip was all about doing things as cheaply as possible. The accommodation was a multi-bed room in a hostel above a coffee shop, a mere hop, skip and a jump over a canal away from the red light district. I thought we might have had to bunk up but I didn't expect for us all to sleep in the same room. The thought of being in full socialising mode all of the time was daunting. I needed, at the very least, half an hour in the morning to wrestle myself into that particular costume and pull down that particular mask, preferably while doom scrolling my Facebook feed on the toilet while my legs went numb without people queuing outside of the door waiting for me. My bladder was shy at the best of times and was sure to protest at that level of performance anxiety. Neither was I enamoured by the thought of trying to sleep in a room full of farting, snoring drunkards above a banging coffee-shop.

I didn't want to go. In an effort to fool myself that it would be fun and decadent I decided to start early. On the way to the hotel at the airport I stopped in M&S at the station and treated myself to a small, expensive gorge. I reasoned that I wouldn't be seeing anything approaching healthy food for the foreseeable future and thought a little something was in order before the ordeal I was about to endure. As soon as I'd dropped my bags into the hotel room I'd tipped the food containers onto the bed, surveying the plethora of colours and textures. It wasn't a binge, it was a treat I told myself.

Getting comfortable on the wide, springy bed I'd peeled back the film on the first pot and dropped a fat sun-dried tomato onto my tongue, savouring the sour burst of juice. Following it had been a pearl of creamy mozzarella. Next a packet of edamame beans, then bright red peppers – roasted and soft, followed by juicy olives stuffed with garlic, eating faster and faster. I'd eaten piggishly, stuffing leaves and vegetables into my mouth, dipping my fingers into bowls and sucking the olive oil or dressing from them, making little huffs of enjoyment through the food in my mouth. It was something

Amelia had chastised me about many times. I'd wiped my greasy, aromatic fingers on my legs, smearing the flesh and hair with flecks of herbs suspended in oil, swirling it like body paint. I ended the abandon by chugging at a bottle of pulpy orange juice, not worrying as some of it sluiced down my chin and into my chest hair. In raptures I'd closed my eyes, luxuriating in abandon and bad manners. It didn't make me feel any better. I just felt remorseful and incredibly full.

After taking a quick shower to wash off the signs of my gluttonous feast, I'd settled back into the nest I had made in the bed, and began my second indulgence; YouTube videos. The next couple of hours were spent engaging in another kind of binge; video after video of Amsterdam walking tours, red light walking tours, bike tours and Segway tours while rubbing my bulging stomach. Unlike the food there was no natural stopping point, no end in sight, there would never be an end to available videos. My eyes were sore and drooping as I pressed, next, next, next.

Finally I managed to sleep but the wake-up call from the front desk seemed to trill in the room almost as soon as I had closed my eyes. The smells from all of the packages in the open waste paper basket made me feel nauseous. I was as sick from the food as I was from the regret and neither feelings were helped by the rolling motion of the airport transfer bus as I tried to make my way to a seat. My phone beeped. The group chat was replete with ecstatic, multi-exclamation-marked messages from my friends who obviously were not regretting their decision to attend.

It seemed that last night, while I had been falling down my YouTube rabbit hole of influencer led commentary and shaky camera work to buoy my spirits, the rest of the lads were as excited and expectant as kids on Christmas Day. There were a couple of selfies this morning from Keith and Tommy, looking suitably small-eyed from being awake at such an early hour. The phrase 'piss holes in the snow' came to mind. As I kept scrolling a jubilant message from Ross popped up, saying he'd secured a table in the airport pub. It was accompanied by a picture; a line of shots along the bar, against the background of the sun barely rising through the window onto the runway. My stomach clenched mutinously. Not being a big fan of shots at the best of times, a breakfast shot on a perilously full stomach seemed beyond the pale. Attempting to swallow my trepidation and acid reflux, I typed out an equally exclamation-mark-laden message, stating that I was on the way and would be with him shortly. My thumb hovered over the send button. If I delayed sending the message for a little while I could dally in the terminal, maybe read the back of some books, buy some antacids, before meeting up with Ross in the bar. It would hopefully stop the awkward situation of being the only two in attendance, having to make small talk until the rest of the lads turned up. Sighing, annoyed at myself and my reticence I pressed send, resigned to trying to make the effort this weekend. I plastered a smile on my face and watched the terminal coming ever closer through the condensation streaked windows.

Thankfully my fears at being the first one there with only Ross for company were unfounded. As I approached through the streams of other travellers, dodging wheelie suitcases and small, fractious children, I saw Stuart sitting in front of a nearly full pint. His face was a pale shade of green. Obviously, the thought of breakfast booze wasn't edifying to him either and certainly wasn't going down easily. Ross on the other hand, was almost bouncing off the walls with excitement. His eyes were already glassy and I noted the small collection of empty shot glasses in front of him. Great. If I wasn't exhausted enough from a lack of sleep and the early morning wake up call I was now going to be dealing with a hyperactive toddler of a man who was soon going to be obnoxiously, embarrassingly drunk on a metal tube with no means of escape. My back teeth ground together automatically.

"Joe-Joe, how you doing?!" Ross bellowed,

prompting a few bleary eyed passengers to eyeball him from the seating area outside of the pub. Before I had a chance to attempt a cheery answer he was thrusting a carrier bag into my arms, grinning his best shit-eating grin. The one that usually meant you were going to have to good naturedly endure something that made you want to punch him in the face. One of my back molars protested at the further clenching of my jaw.

I opened the bag with trepidation and pulled out an over sized t-shirt. Not just over sized, the shirt was so large it would have had to have been specifically ordered from a speciality store. It had obviously too optimistic of me to assume that Ross hadn't picked up on my sensitivities around weight and exercise. Unfurling the sail-like T-shirt I noticed it had an inscription on the back 'Stu's Stags' followed by the date and then, in bright red letters, several inches tall and emblazoned across the whole of the back of the shirt it read 'Jonah "The Whale" Brigham'. My stomach dropped to my knees. It was a literal nightmare in sartorial form. The urge to drop the bag on the floor, turn around and leave the airport without a further word was so strong it was making my hands shake. Only a sense of duty and politeness kept me rooted to the spot. Ross looked at my shocked face and brayed, tears of mirth squirting from the corners of his eyes. He leaned on his knees, slapping them as hard as any pantomime hero, squawking with delight at my face. I looked round, appalled, at Stuart who shrugged with a now all too familiar sheepish smile, avoiding my eyes. That bastard. That pair of bastards. My face was taut with barely suppressed rage as I pulled the enormous t-shirt over my head. It swamped me, slipping down my thighs and past my elbows. I reached for one of the shot glasses, knocking it back quickly, the liquid burning deep down with my fury. Fuck it, I thought, Self-medication here I come.

I'd desperately not wanted Ross to know my full name, I couldn't stand the thought of that most vulnerable part of me between his razor sharp teeth. But he was as adept at finding weakness as a pig snuffling out truffles and to me this truffle was an absolute doozy. Do you remember that episode of *The Simpsons* when Marge and Homer are deciding what to call Bart before he is born? Marge states a name choice and Homer explains to her what brutal nickname the kids would give him at school if they chose it. Ignoring the fact that Bart definitely would have been called Fart Simpson by British school kids, I really wish that my parents had done something similar before coming to the decision to call me Jonah. I've heard so many Jonah and the whale jokes that it would be my specialist subject were I ever to appear on *Mastermind*.

The first time I'd heard the biblical story of

Jonah and the whale was during a primary school R.E lesson. Even now I can still remember the heat in my face as it went crimson and blotchy while listening to the story of my name-sake being vomited up by a whale because he was trying to run away from God, like a big coward. I remember the gleeful faces of my classmates as they cast furtive glances back at me, miming sticking their fingers down their throats while I was trapped listening to a story that I knew was going to be used against me for many, many playtimes to come. Have you read the story of Jonah and the whale? Spoiler alert but Jonah does not come out of it looking great. Jonah is not only a coward but also the kind of man happy to let the women and children of Nineveh all die just so he doesn't look like a false prophet. He is not one of the good guys. Nobody wants to be named after one of the bad guys. So not only did I assume that I was named after a coward but the name always brought up a plethora of fat jokes. Try not having an issue with your weight after that!

The story made me embarrassed but also furious. I was, of course, apoplectic at the teacher who had decided it appropriate to read that story. I mean he was a teacher, he saw everyday how mean kids were so why did he pick that particular story to read? Did he have a grudge against me? Had I been too well rounded and confident a child thus far, so he'd decided to knock me down a couple of pegs?

However, I was also enraged at my parents for not only naming me the same as this person but for never warning me about the connotations of the name. They let me be blind-sided and left to a deafening crescendo of vomit noises and whale song in the playground that continued for years. I went home with hot, angry tears on my cheeks and shouted at my mother as soon as my book bag hit the hall carpet. I didn't stop crying, even when my dad tried to tell me about how I'd actually been named after Jonah Jones the jazz trumpeter.

My dad was a jazz freak and it had been the soundtrack of my childhood, but I never knew the complicated rhythms and soaring crescendos would result in an almost entire childhood of bullying. To add insult to injury, my brother Miles, also named after a famous jazz trumpeter had none of the same problems. No self image issues in his future. He was able to properly enjoy my mother's cooking and with no burning need to exercise, unlike me, he became quite proficient in the art of playing *Tomb Raider* with one hand and eating crisps with the other. Standing next to each other we looked like Laurel and Hardy. The irony was not lost on me that out of both of us, I did not look like the obvious contender for whale jokes.

I held my breath, waiting for Ross to add insult onto injury with the first of his whale jokes but he was distracted by the feat of drinking as much as humanly possible before our gate was called instead. As predicted, he was a complete and unbelievable nightmare during the entirety of the flight. Before leaving for the gate he had systematically finished off the rest of the drinks left on the table by everyone else in our party. Most of whom, like Stuart and me, were struggling to finish so much alcohol before breakfast. Once on the flight, he couldn't seem to sit still. The flight attendants had to tell him several times to take his seat as he staggered down the aisle between us. Tommy, who had a child of his own, tried all of the tricks in his parental repertoire to corral Ross like his own toddler. In the end buying him yet more alcohol from the drinks trolley seemed to be the only thing that would keep him seated and satiated, much like the old wives' tale of dipping a dummy in brandy to coax a child to sleep. I saw the side-eye glance the stewardess gave her colleague but evidently the thought of what a handful he would be should she not serve him seemed to win out. I wanted to apologise to them on his behalf but knew it would be a bad idea to do so.

Instead of subduing him, the alcohol acted as fuel to his bad behaviour. He became more and more excited, and more and more annoying. By the time we landed it was obvious that it wasn't just me who was getting tired of him. He didn't seem to notice, or if he did he didn't care. After disembarking, I walked behind him as he strode through Schiphol airport with his arms in the air, chanting a football song that started along the lines of "Stu's stags are..." and then degenerated into a lot of slurred oi's and yells. People were looking at us in disgust, thinking us the typical British lager lout stag do. I couldn't blame them but nonetheless my whole body prickled in embarrassment. I wondered briefly if I could turn around and get on the next flight back, and whether anyone would notice. There was bound to be a fight soon. I could be home and in my own bed by tonight. The temptation was strong but instead I followed the group out of the airport and into the weak December sun.

Like a team of sheep dogs, blocking him in from different sides, we manoeuvred Ross out to the bus stop. Once we had him in place I volunteered to go back into the airport to buy the tickets. It gave me a few, blessed minutes of quiet, enough to rub my sore eyes and stubbled cheeks. I tried rolling the tension out of my neck while waiting in the queue, the tendons of my neck creaking like wire cables. Personally I would have quite liked to have experienced the train. Trains are always better on holiday. They always seem to be somehow cleaner and more efficient than those at home. I would have also liked to have seen Centraal Station. I had been reading about it in my guide book the night before. The architecture sounded fascinating. Just one more thing to miss out on.

The bus had arrived by the time I'd walked back into the chilly air in front of the airport. I could hear Ross whooping and laughing as soon as the sliding doors opened. The faces framed in the bus windows were not happy ones. We hadn't even gotten on yet, and they were already tired of Ross's shit. Walking straight onto the bus I gave the little handful of tickets to the driver, gesturing back towards our group who were nudging Ross up the stairs and down the aisle towards the seat. The bus driver looked as unimpressed as I felt.

"Bedankt," I said to the bus driver, using one of the very few Dutch words I'd remembered from the travel guide. It was a shame it didn't have the phrase for "I'm sorry a member of my group is an absolute penis."

Walking to the back of the bus, I averted my eyes from the other passengers, and sat heavily next to John. Ross and Stuart were together in the row next to me, as they had been in the pub and on the plane. They seemed to be joined at the hip. I could see Ross out of the corner of my eye pulling a rubbery, gormless face, which I assumed was meant to be me. He came up beside me, hands pressed together earnestly.

"Oh danke danke Herr Bus Driver," he said into my ear, little shards of spittle tickling the inner cornice as he mocked me.

"That's German, not Dutch," I informed him. I knew as soon as the words left my mouth that I shouldn't have said them. I sounded like a teacher, even to my own spittle soaked ear.

"You're such a swot Jonah," he said rolling his eyes "This is meant to be a lads' weekend, not a school trip," he said, looking back at the others trying to get them to join in on the mockery. Stuart snorted a short laugh and my face began to colour with embarrassment.

I felt like a kid listening to vomiting noises on the playground all over again. Thankfully, he was the only one. The others were too tired and too irritated to get involved. When Ross saw no-one else was joining in, he went back to rummaging around in his bag, looking for the litre of duty free vodka he'd bought in the airport. He began offering it around like he hadn't just tried to get everyone to gang up on me. He was a master of gaslighting.

"Just manners," I said quietly, almost under my breath, hoping that my annoyance and my upset didn't show on my face.

Ross would be interminable for the rest of the day and probably the rest of the holiday if I blew my top so early on but I was furious and hurt and tired. I'd practised keeping the emotion from my face in the steaming bathroom mirror last night, making my expression placid and neutral while intoning obscenities in a calm voice. There was no way I was going to stop being polite, just because Ross thought it was uncool. However, I decided that geeking out to anyone else in the group about architecture or museums was a sure fire way of being summarily humiliated for the entire trip.

I kept thinking about the videos on YouTube last night. The majority of them were narrated by bright, young, fresh faced kids (everyone looked like a kid to me since I'd gone past thirty) straight to camera, babbling overenthusiastically about whatever excursion they were participating in. I decided to do the same. Not on YouTube but in my own head, a running commentary on the holiday, hoping that it might keep me amused. It would also let me voice some of the snarky comments I was trying to bottle up, even if that voicing would only be in my own head. A pressure valve release to stop me flipping my lid.

"Ladies and gentlemen, here we have the

common or garden stag do, complete with the genus *lagerus loutus*, not dissimilar from the species *footballus hooliganus*. On your right you will see Amsterdam Centraal station, designed by Pierre Cuypers and opened in 1889. Did you know it has a forty metre cast iron platform roof? From here we're going to get the number fourteen tram. As we travel down Damrak you will see the Sexmueseum Amsterdam, the world's first and oldest sex museum. On the right, you will see in the distance De Oude Kerk: Amsterdam's oldest building, a Church consecrated in 1302 and now housing an art gallery. Wild right? Back on your right you will see Bodyworks; awesome if you want to see a corpse riding another corpse in reverse cowgirl, and of course here's KFC. Now watch as our herd of *loutus* remove themselves from the tram, searching for food and shelter."

It was a bit more David Attenborough than hip and trendy travel vlogger but that was probably more down to my age than anything else. I was having so much fun with my internal nature documentary slash travel video commentary that I almost missed John tugging my sleeve to let me know everyone else was nearly off the tram. I wondered whether I could really make it a thing, be Insta or YouTube famous. Quit the day job and make it big online. I could call the show 'Stag Dos For Introverts' or 'How To Travel With People You

Hate'. The duty free vodka had been passed around since we left the airport. It could be said that most of our group's disembarkation from the tram onto the busy street was less than graceful due to its effects. I'd been tipping the bottle back against my closed lips every time it was handed to me. It meant I only got the wonderful astringent taste of vodka on my lips, like a methylated spirit flavoured lip balm, and none of the disorderly side effects. I was still sober enough to work out where the hell we were, and where the hell we were going. The best man was in no fit state to work out directions and I'm not even sure the stag knew which country we were in.

"No man left behind," Ross shrieked, making a passing woman cringe from the volume of his voice in her ear. I really wished we could leave Ross behind but Stuart, his new bestie, probably wouldn't hear of it. I rolled my eyes at their departing backs.

Our little group tottered and stumbled, lunged and plunged through the busy streets of the red light district. I felt like a teacher on a field trip, telling the little ones to hold onto their buddies so they didn't get lost. More than once I saw one of them veer dangerously close to the lip of the canal. I found myself soothing and cajoling, moving the vulnerable little group on, telling them not to trip other people on the streets with their suitcases and holdalls. I desperately wanted to make it to the hostel without one of them hurling themselves or a member of the general public into the water. That, and the early morning, was leaving my nerves perilously close to fully fraying. I had promised myself, and Amelia, that I was going to be happy-go-lucky, laid back and just one of the guys this weekend. Instead I was starting to feel like my father who always, without fail, yelled at my brother and me that if we didn't stop our caterwauling he would turn this car right around and take us back home thank you very much. It always managed to shut us up but I doubted it would have the same affect on a ramshackle group of inebriated men in their thirties. I'd just end up embarrassing myself. Again.

Using the map in the back of the guidebook, I took us an alternative way to the hostel. I didn't think I had the strength of will, or the patience, to get everyone past the temptation of the windows in the red light district. I'd read that they were manned, or womanned I guess, even in the daytime. Personally I would have been more than happy to avoid the red light district all together. I knew we were going to visit. I was more than eighty percent sure that one of our group was going to stop in on one of the establishments and more than ninety percent certain that when I got home Amelia was going to question me on it. I would be torn between the 'What Goes On Tour Stays On Tour' mentality required of a boys weekend, and the unerring honesty I always strived for in my relationship. I knew I would also be full of the second hand guilt of being privy to someone else engaging in something that I personally thought was wrong. I was terrified that guilty look would show on my face and scare Amelia into thinking that I myself had indulged in some extracurricular activities. You know that feeling when the police drive past and you sit bolt upright in your seat checking your seatbelt and your mirrors, convinced you're going to get pulled over, even if you haven't done anything wrong? Or when you walk through airport security convinced they are going to find a kilo of cocaine in your shaving kit that you never knew was there. That was how I felt. I knew I wasn't going to betray her but I didn't want the fear and guilt to be an expression on my face on my return, and make her think otherwise.

I could have cried when we finally got to our accommodation. I was so relieved that we had made it without major incident. The hostel stood next to the canal on a road set between two gently curving bridges. It was a beautiful street, picture postcard perfect. Even though the day had been hard so far, there was a small thrill at being somewhere new and so aesthetically pleasing. Turning to the front of the building I felt that thrill dull a couple of notches.

Even though the day was still early, the neon illuminated downstairs lounge bar was full of people drinking, playing pool and watching sport on the televisions. It was loud and bright and I was more than aware that the sleeping quarters were going to be above all that commotion. I was glad I had packed earplugs.

My herd of cats made their way straight to the bar and kept on going where they left off in the airport, on the plane, on the bus and on the tram. I made my way to the reception desk and dealt with the necessary formalities – keys, details of how to get in after hours, house rules, deposits etc. I took my bags and made my way up to the dorms. Luckily there didn't seem to be any strangers already in situ. I claimed one of the bottom bunks and dropped my bags on the scratchy, utilitarian looking blanket to secure my spot, like putting your towel on a sunbed. I sat for a moment, the mattress groaning a little at my weight. It was good to take a moment. I sat for a while, breathing in the smell of a well trafficked bedroom, and tried to separate my feelings from my facial expression, like a cop directing rubberneckers from an accident scene. Taking a deep breath and plastering a smile onto my sleep deprived face, I made my way back downstairs to the bar. Stuart's stags had landed.

**

That airport pub often pops up in my thoughts. I wonder what would have happened had I gone with my gut and walked away when Ross gave me that shirt. I wouldn't have been in Amsterdam at the time. The most innocuous dreams I have are about that pub, dreams where I walk away, dreams about how I stayed. When the evacuation flight landed back in the UK, the small number of other survivors and I were taken directly from the plane by a group of soldiers. They walked us across the runway and into the darkened airport which had been closed, we were told, as a precautionary measure. At least there were no queues at passport control. It wasn't clear if the precaution was for us or for the general public. They led us through the silent airport, past shuttered shops and the pub we'd drunk in before we left. The chairs and stools on the tables stood like silent sentinels as we walked past. An empty airport is an unnatural place. The military told us they would be holding us for a while, another precaution they said. They also wished to 'debrief' us. I didn't realise debriefing was a euphemism for two days of interrogation, to wring every last detail out of us.

They settled us in a conference room somewhere in the bowels of the airport. It was somewhere the general public was never meant to see and it was definitely not set up for habitation. The army had pushed the chairs and tables to the edges of the room and laid out some camp beds and blow up mattresses. One poor soul had to make do with a lilo, presumably from one of the gift shops within the airport. Its jaunty colours were a horrible juxtaposition against the ugly, industrial carpet and the horror that loomed in the room like a spectre.

They took us, one by one, to use the bathrooms, to sponge dried blood off our skin with wet paper towels which fell apart into bloody, pulpy messes in the sink. I turned off all the lights but one when it was my turn. I couldn't bear to see my reflection in the bank of mirrors and after so much time without sleep my eyes were red rimmed and sensitive to the harsh lights. But I couldn't stand it to be fully dark. I now knew what lurked in the darkness. I managed what I had once heard called a whore's bath; a quick sink wash with a handful of wet paper towels and soap from the dispenser. I felt vulnerable and humiliated, clothed only in my underwear and with a soldier waiting at the door. I had renewed sympathy for the feelings of prison inmates.

When I knocked on the door the soldier pushed a pile of fresh clothes of wildly differing sizes into my arms. I dressed myself in a XXXXXL t-shirt adorned with silently baying wolves and shiny nylon trousers that were so short that they were practically peddle pushers. The soldier who had given me the incongruous fashion choices took my bloody and torn clothing and stuffed each piece into sealable evidence bags. He told me I could claim back my belongings once the military's investigation had been completed. I didn't bother taking the slip from him. There was no way I wanted the personal reminders of the worst period of my life back. What was I going to do, pop them into the washing machine with a good slug of bleach, hoping they'd be good enough to wear back down the pub again?

After being given new clothes, pre-packaged food and bottles of water from the airport's food court. we were separated and left to wait until our time for interrogation. I'm not sure why they separated us. I don't know if they were worried about collaboration or simply concerned about the threat that a group of stressed out, tired, angry and traumatised people posed to a small number of soldiers in a part of the airport not even currently being used by aviation staff. That or they were worried about the threat of infection. Little did they know I had already collaborated on a story - the whitewash train had long left my own personal station, way before I had even gotten on the plane. I didn't mind being on my own. I'd done the getting to know you small talk with strangers once already during this crisis. It had not gone well. I had no inclination to try it again.

I told the soldiers most of what I knew. I told them up one side and down the other, but they kept on asking and asking and asking. They probably knew I was holding back details. The tenuous hold I had on my temper and sanity was fraying with the constant questions, but I held fast and continued to keep back pieces of my story. They were mine after all, nobody could make me share them. Keep it vague, I said over and over again in my head, a running loop. When it was over, when they had bled me dry of any information that might be of any use to them, they pushed a pen and paper over to me and asked for the details of someone to come and collect me. At the time I was glad it was the soldiers making the calls and that they hadn't given me a phone for me to call myself. I had no idea what I would have said once I heard Amelia's voice on the line.

"Hi honey, great news, I survived the disaster you've probably been watching on the TV. I'm at the airport and I need a ride. Can you pick me up? No you won't be picking me up from the normal place. You'll have to follow the armed personnel to an undisclosed part of the airport. How am I? Well I've seen and done things I'll never forget, So, not

great? Reckon we can talk about it later though? After the armed guards let me out of the interrogation room I've been in for the last two days? Thanks babe! Bring snacks!"

There would be no welcome-back banners held by family members or loved ones waiting expectantly in the arrival lounge. I didn't want to think about the families who were going to be waiting on the tarmac for their loved ones arriving in body bags. Or the families whose loved ones would not be coming home at all. I remember Amelia's pale face, illuminated by the loading dock lights, as they let me out of a strange back exit to meet her. I remember the tightness of her grasp as she threw herself into my arms, clinging on to me so hard she left little crescent moon bruises on the backs of my arms. I was already so black and blue that I didn't notice a few more added to the collection. I don't remember the drive back home. I was so exhausted that I got into the back seat and slipped into a sleep that was more like unconsciousness for the whole journey.

Once we got home, I just about managed to strip off the borrowed, emergency clothing and take a scalding hot shower. I was barely managing to stand upright but I could not get into our bed smelling of old blood, fear sweat and industrial hand wash from my sink bath. Amelia handed me a towel as I got out of the shower but, seeing me swaying dangerously on the bath mat, took the towel back and gently dried my body, avoiding all of the bruises and scrapes as best she could. She pulled a clean t-shirt over my head and let me hold on to her shoulders while I put my legs through a pair of tracksuit bottoms. It reminded me of being dressed for bed as a little kid. In that moment, tired and emotional, I wanted my mum more than anything else. Swallowing back tears I climbed into our bed and Amelia climbed in next to me. She spooned her body around mine, infusing it with her heat, and held me until I dropped back into unconsciousness. It was the last full night I've had.

CHAPTER SEVEN: JENNIFER

The scream cut through the loud burble of the crowd, piercing and shrill, the loudest thing I had ever heard. We're pack animals at heart, we know what real danger sounds like. We might be pretty high up on the food chain but we're not immune to being killed and/or eaten by something bigger or meaner than us. The high, keening scream of someone in actual trouble seemed to freeze all the blood in my veins, rooting me to the spot. Like a frightened gazelle, I was trying to work out where the danger was coming from and which way to run. I couldn't see anything, only the backs of people's bodies as they stood in front of me, the shocked faces on the bridge above. I didn't see the creature grab the woman's ankle. I didn't see it drag her over the stone lip, into the frothing, swirling mass of mouths and teeth and fury. But I heard it. It was impossible not to. The sound of it rendered the crowd silent. It sliced through the air, changing from surprise to the rising cadence of pain and then the paroxysms of agony, before gurgling away, filling with water as the creatures dragged her below. I heard the silence as she was dragged under the surface. But still I heard the crunching.

The crowd surged backwards, almost as one

entity, desperate to get away from the canal and the carnage within. Fear reduces us to our baser instincts - there is no politeness or empathy, only a primal urge to save one's own skin. The crowd pushed and pulled and crushed against one another, hair yanked, clothes ripped and nails raked over flesh. It became an unmovable force, not stopping if anyone on the periphery fell under its thunderous movement. The crush was peppered with shrieks of the fallen.

I pushed my way to the side of the throng, popping out the other side like a cork forced from a bottle, out of the way of its trampling feet. Others were not so lucky. I saw the rolling whites of a man's eye as he disappeared under the scrum. The crack of someone's fingers underfoot was loud in my ear. The swell of people knocked into a food truck on the bridge, made it rock ominously as more and more people became trapped against its metal sides. Finally it tipped, splattering the pavement with the sharp, salty smell of raw herring, diced onions and condiments. The little fish were smashed underfoot, creating a slippery carpet of mush, that saw more people sliding under the crush of the crowd. The air was thick with the briny scent of fish and blood.

The jostling, skittering crowd knocked more people into the water. They fell over the railings lining the bridge, some holding on for precious seconds before losing their grip and tumbling into the water below. Some were shoved straight over the sides of the canal's lip, having no chance to find anything to grip onto. They fell directly into the feeding frenzy below. Water-logged hands, sloughing slipped skin, gripped onto their limbs and pulled them into a death roll as gruesome and effective as that of any crocodilian. The screaming was ubiquitous, reverberating against my eardrums. I pushed my hands against my ears but it did nothing to dull the sound.

Those who'd fallen into the water were being torn apart by the creatures. A frothing chum of flesh, bone and clothes was already floating down the canal, the creatures too frenzied to consume all of their prey in one go. Those who had fallen and been crushed near the lip of the canal were being used by the creatures not actively eating to pull themselves up onto the pavement. Clawed hands dug into living, screaming flesh, slithering up the slick wall and onto the road. They threw themselves forward into the rapidly retreating crowd. Some fell upon the prone victims in an ecstasy of feeding, torn sinews and hot blood splattered across the pavement. They stood for a moment, heads whipping back and forth, seemingly overwhelmed by the choice of meals running for their lives over the bridges and down the streets. Some were running as soon as they made it out of the steep canal basin. All of them were fast. Very, very fast.

I might have stood with my hands pressed against my ears, frozen with fear, until one of the creatures found me and sunk its teeth into my pale flesh, ending my life right then and there. But someone slipped, thudding into me, the sharp point of their elbow finding my eye, clenched shut against the horror unfolding before me. The force sent me tumbling onto the floor, skinning both of my palms as I tried to save myself. The startling pain of both my skinned hands and my rapidly swelling eye got me moving. Scrambling to my feet I began running to where I had left the bike, what seemed like hours ago but was probably only minutes. Pulling the heavy frame towards me, I felt it bash painfully into my hip. I managed to lift myself onto the high seat and push off but panic had completely removed the little balance I'd previously had. Immediately I fell, the side of my face hitting the hard pavement. My mouth filled with the salty copper gush of blood from my bitten tongue. Gibbering with fear, I managed to pull the heavy bike upright and got back on, pushing all of my strength onto the metal pedals.

More and more of the creatures were now in the crowd, grabbing and clawing. They pulled victims in close, to clamp their bloodied jaws onto arms and necks and faces. A dead hand, with shattered fingernails, skimmed the back of my neck as I peddled past, adrenaline fizzing in my muscles and tears running down my face. I was just a whisker too quick for it, and its nails trailed uselessly down my back. I thought I could smell its breath as it lunged for me, but that could have just been the raw herring. Thinking I was free and away in the wind I did not expect another pair of hands to alight on my body. These were definitely human and certainly found purchase, pushing me unceremoniously from the saddle of the bike. The ground came up to meet me hard. My knees and elbows lost at least one layer of skin, my poor skinned hands losing a few more. They now more closely resembled raw hamburger meat than human appendages. Turning my head I managed to see my assailant through my good eye, all hipster beard and beanie hat, pulling my stolen bike up roughly. He shrugged at me and got on, moving away at speed. No honour among thieves it seemed.

I'd managed to get a little way ahead of the crowd but they were coming up behind me. Both in its wake and entwined within the crowd were the creatures, weaving in and out, like a pack of wild dogs, pulling anyone to the ground who came into their grasp. I wasn't fast. As much as adrenaline might help, I was still overweight with a tendency to wheeze when faced with any intense cardio.

There was no way I was going to outrun them. I had to find another way to escape the wave of death coming towards me.

**

My life has been very different since returning from Amsterdam. In contrast to so many of the others in the airport, there was no-one there to pick me up after the soldier's de-briefing. There was no weeping partner or concerned family member. I didn't want any of my friends to see me like that. I didn't want to have to explain or be at the mercy of anyone else ever again. So I went home. Alone. All that was waiting for me in my flat was some spoiled milk and an electricity bill on the mat. I didn't go back to my old job. I just never returned, not bothering to even contact my boss. They probably thought I had never made it back from Amsterdam. I didn't care if they thought I was dead. I didn't care that my favourite mug on still my desk or that the Anderson report that was due upon my return would never be finished. I didn't care that I would never see any of my co-workers again or that it would make for a poor reference by not even bothering to resign from the job I'd been in for over a decade. I just didn't care about it. Any of it. At all. It seemed so utterly unimportant.

I sat in my flat, lights blazing and didn't talk to anyone. I logged off social media. Permanently. My groceries were ordered online with a note to ring the bell and leave the bags outside. The same with any take-out or online shopping. I simply didn't talk to anyone and it was making me strange. After weeks of not uttering a word to another soul it became obvious, if I didn't want to become a weird hermit lady, that I had to get back out there and re-enter society in some way. So when the committee reached out to me, asking me to do a talk about my experiences, I thought it was a sign. I actually felt a little hopeful.

That hope is starting to dim somewhat. During my retelling of the first time I saw the creatures, and the way they tore into the crowd like a starving man into a bag of peanuts, I realise that being alone so much has certainly turned me a bit odd. The faces in this crowd, standing out in the darkened auditorium, are horrified at my account. The images have been so a constant companion to me that I think I am desensitised to how shocking the description might be to others. There is the sound of quiet retching somewhere in the back. It's too late now. Ignoring it, I carry on.

CHAPTER EIGHT: JONAH

Now that I had gotten rid of last night's dinner, a plate of fried bar snacks shared between us most of which had ended up on the floor, and my stomach had recalibrated I was suddenly quite hungry. Ross had no idea where to go so I directed us to the square at Rembrandtplein, sure that it would have plenty of options for breakfast. Thankfully it wasn't far, as I wasn't the only one struggling that morning. Rembrandtplein was a strange mix of the old and the new. On one side were the traditional, skinny, dark brown buildings synonymous with Amsterdam. On the other side of the square was a Starbucks. I didn't think anyone was in a fit state for me to tell them about the origins of the cast iron statue of Rembrant, which sits in the middle of the square, or how it is one of the oldest surviving public statues in Amsterdam. Honestly, I wasn't sure how much I really cared either. I cared much more about coffee and sitting down. I steered the group away from the Starbucks and onto the more traditional side of the road.

Installing ourselves en masse in one of the cafes I ordered something greasy, hoping it would go to work on my hangover. The cup of coffee that came with it was scorching and tar-like, coating my tongue, which still felt fuzzy despite the mouthwash. It did the trick, working its magic on my puffy, pin-pricked eyes, opening them up so my visage more closely resembled a normal human face, rather than a victim of a multitude of bee stings. Everyone else ordered beers. As we sat around the breakfast table, discussing the plans for the day, I started to feel a bit more present in the land of the living. With that renewed sentience came guilt about my grumpiness of the day before. I resolved anew to get into the spirit of the thing. Feeling much more optimistic and less likely to chunder I ordered a beer to join in with the others. Once it was placed down in front of me on the tablecloth, already heavily stained by a group of men with limited table manners, my eye caught Stuart's. He winked at me and smiled. I was glad I was trying hard to fit in. I wanted to do that for my friend. I didn't see the look Stuart gave to the others around the table as I drank heartily from the first beer of the day.

We bar hopped our way back towards the red light district from Rembrandtsplein. Passing close to the Bloemenmarkt, I experienced a pang of longing. I'd read about it in my guidebook and would have loved to have seen it but leaving the bar crawl to go look at flowers was more than my life was worth. I might as well have thrown myself straight into the canal. As we got closer and closer to the red light district, I became more and more nervous. I knew what we were heading back to - those windows and the brothels behind them. It was like a homing beacon for Ross. I found myself buying more rounds. Anything to keep us in the bars for longer, and away from that potential for trouble. I tried several tactics to keep us away from that place. I bought more and more beers to keep the group malleable and changed bars often, edging us away from the red light district. Seemingly immune to the effects of massive quantities of alcohol Ross managed to counter every move, edging us closer again. It was like a game of chess and I was losing. I couldn't win. So I gave up. I was tired and more than a little drunk and wasn't the only one. The rest of the guys, tripped and stumbled from the exit of the bar, like a group of excited puppies, not sure where to pin their inebriated focus. As they huddled on the pavement, waiting for further instructions, the windows of the red light district winked in the afternoon sun.

The distant glinting was like the appearance of a mirage in the desert, a sparkling oasis for thirsty travellers. The group of men almost ran towards them. Only myself and Tommy held back. I know we weren't the only ones with partners. We just seemed to be the only ones who'd remembered they existed. In any case I found the sight of women in little glass cubes distasteful. It reminded me of a vending machine; a line of products lined up, until someone comes along with the right change. It made me hot and embarrassed, like I needed to apologise to them all. The feeling of their eyes on me only inflamed my shame. I watched the others crowding around the windows, loudly extolling the virtue of this lady's assets over the others, posturing and gesturing at the women within. The group of excited puppies had become a pack of salivating dogs and the pack mentality was getting their blood up. You could almost smell it in the cold afternoon air.

"So come on lads, who's up for it? Eh? Eh?" shouted Ross, his stance wide and his eyes glassy with beer and lust. "What happens on tour, stays on tour boys!" he roared, banging his hairy fist against his chest. He reminded me of the old black and white *King Kong* movies; a great, inarticulate beast beating his fists, yelling and trying to scoop up unsuspecting women into his hairy paws.

His slightly blurry focus flitted across the group, looking for takers and grazing across my face. My distaste must have been evident, pockmarked on my skin like acne scars. I saw Ross's mouth pull up in an ugly sneer.

"You're such a snowflake Jonah," he hissed, his hot spittle almost sizzling in the cold air. The obvious dislike of me bubbled up onto his normally nonchalant, sarcastic face. It was like another person coming to the surface. Stuart walked past him and stood next to me and the vitriol slid off Ross's face so fast I thought I had imagined it.

"Come on Stu, one last shag for the road mate?" He called over to Stuart, suddenly gregarious again, winking at him in a reptilian manner. I stood gawping at them both, not sure if I had imagined the previous exchange.

Stuart shuffled awkwardly, looking at his feet and didn't reply. I didn't understand. The Stuart I knew and went to school with stood up for his convictions, and didn't worry about looking 'cool'. We'd been terminally uncool at school, not part of the main crowd and, I thought, happy about it. But now Stuart had joined in with the cool kids in his new office and it seemed to be making him conflicted about his own values. The Stuart I thought I knew would never dream of cheating on his fiance just to keep up appearances with someone like Ross. I nudged his shoulder with mine.

"You don't have to do this you know," I said to him quietly out of the side of my mouth, angling my face away from Ross, who hadn't seemed to notice anyway. His focus was back on the women in the windows.

"Shit Jonah. I dunno. Once you get married its the same girl forever isn't it? Would it really be so bad to have one last experience before settling down? But if she finds out she'd be crushed. I dunno what to do here mate," Stuart said, rubbing his face. A day and a half of heavy drinking and a moral conundrum seemed to be taking its toll. He suddenly looked old. I could feel the existential crisis of my own fleeting youth fluttering somewhere behind my sternum.

"I'll sort it," I told him, bumping up against his shoulder more jovially than I felt.

This stag do was turning into a shit-show. Weren't they meant to be fun? I wished we'd just gone away to a seaside B&B for a night or one big blow out at the pub and had done with it. I felt like the guy spinning plates at the circus, trying to keep everyone happy and in the air. Like the perpetual people pleaser, I had taken on the role without a second thought. It was exhausting.

I looked around desperately, trying to think of a solution. It came to me in gaudy, neon letters.

"What about that?" I said quietly to Stuart, gesturing over to the building with a slight inclination of my head, trying not to garner too much attention from the others. The front of the building shouted 'LIVE SEX. GIRLS, GIRLS, GIRLS. PEEPS SHOWS' in foot high letters. It looked like my idea of hell but I thought it might be a way for the others to get their kicks without visiting the brothels. Stuart nodded slightly so I repeated the question for the rest of the group.

"What about that?" I repeated, loud enough to be heard over the wolf whistles and jeers from the group looking into the windows.

A collective cheer went up, eliciting looks of relief from the women now that they wouldn't have to deal with our merry band of salivating punters. Stuart exhaled in relief behind me. I seemed to have found a middle ground to please everyone. Except me of course. The plates kept spinning. A sigh crept from between my own lips into the cold air. I could see it dissipating in a warm mist in front of me.

The foyer of the building was blessedly dark and smelt strongly of industrial strength air freshener. I didn't want to consider for too long about the smells it was trying to cover. The guys split up, some to the strippers upstairs and some to the peep-shows in the back. After they dispersed I found myself standing with Stuart and Ross. The tension between them was palpable, Ross sulking because he couldn't visit one of the brothels, Stuart mad because he'd been put on the spot. I felt like a very awkward child, trying to console two fighting parents by jollying them both along with a stream of fabricated bright chatter and sham smiles.

An announcement came over the PA system that the live show was about to begin. Ross stalked into the main room and, reluctantly, Stuart and I followed behind him. Ross picked the seats closest to the stage. I winced, hoping it wasn't like a comedy night where I might get picked on to participate. Worse, it might be like one of those events that tell the audience that the first three rows might get wet. I hadn't brought my cagoule. As the show started, the realisation that I'd made a terrible mistake crawled over my skin. I should have left them to go to the brothels. I could have wondered off to a museum for a couple of hours and seen some of the beautiful works of art from the grand masters. Instead, I was going to be watching a very bored looking couple shagging on a stage next to my best friend and his friend whom I detested. I was mortified. It was like the equivalent of inviting people to a movie night, and cracking out the porn with the popcorn. Do you remember when you were going through puberty and your body would betray you at every opportunity? Waking up, the bus hitting a pothole, an advert for bras, everything seemed to give me a hard-on as a teenager. I was always terrified that I'd stand up at school with a tell-tale bulge in the front of my nylon uniform trousers and have the whole class laughing at me. I had my mum buy pants two sizes too small whenever she went shopping to make sure everything was secure down there. What happened if my body betrayed me now? As the performers climbed up onto the stage, fully naked, I started to feel the old familiar childhood fear. What happened if I got a bit of a lob on? What happened if everyone saw, if it was the talk of the weekend. The anxiety about it was starting to make me sweat. I leaned over to Stuart.

"I'm going to get some drinks in," I said in my gruffest, manliest voice.

"What's the matter Joe-Joe? Off to the gents already are ya?" leered Ross, leaning towards me.

Heat blossomed in my cheeks but I didn't bother answering him to explain myself, knowing that it would almost certainly make things worse. I'd stammer, blush or muddle my words up as his grin got wider and wider. Standing silently I made my way to the bar at the back of the room and ordered the drinks, making sure not to turn around to face the stage. I couldn't see the performers but I could hear them, their moans and groans straight from the soundtrack of many an x-rated movie. The bartender also didn't meet my eye of which I was glad. Locking eyes with a total stranger over a handful of change and fake sex noise was an embarrassment too far for today. I sipped at the cheap-tasting, but ridiculously expensive, beer and made no move to go back to my seat. I wondered how long I could hide at the bar before Stuart would also think I'd gone to the bathrooms to sort myself out. Irritated I picked up the beers, getting ready to take them back to Stuart and Ross.

I nearly threw the extortionate beers all over the carpet as every single mobile phone in the building, including mine, chirruped at once. It blared out from my pocket with a mechanical shriek I had never heard before. It was all the more shocking because my phone had been on silent mode for the last decade or so and on airplane mode while we'd been in Amsterdam to cut down on roaming charges. Everyone looked down at their phones all at once, like a Mexican wave moving through the crowd. Shakily, I put the beers back down on the bar and looked down at my own screen **'EMERGENCY ALERT – EXTERNAL THREAT TO LIFE. SEEK SHELTER. AWAIT FURTHER INSTRUCTIONS'**. I looked around, desperate for an adult who would tell me what this meant and what I had to do. Instead I saw Tommy walking through the crowd, so intent on his screen he almost bumped into several people. His journey closely resembled a slalom but instead of poles he was dodging sex club patrons turned into statues by their own devices.

"Well that doesn't look good," he muttered when he finally reached me. The understatement of the century. It might have been amusing had I not seen the fear in his face and not felt so petrified myself.

"I've got to ring home. Oh my God. My wife! My kid!" he cried, putting the phone to his ear and jamming a finger in the other to block out the noisy room. Instantly he took the phone away from his head, looking down at it like it had betrayed him.

"No service," he shouted to me over the noise of generalised panic in the building.

I looked down at my own phone, Amelia and me smiling goofily at the screen as my background picture. I'd turned off airplane mode but 'No Service' was still displayed at the top of the screen. No, this wasn't good. It wasn't good at all.

As the chatter increased, stag parties and hen dos shouting to each other about the alert and the lack of service, it became obvious to the performers on stage that absolutely no-one was watching them do the deed. I watched the male performer stand up, his hard-on bobbing up and down comically as he looked around, confused. His partner grabbed a robe from the side of the stage and dug around in its pockets, bringing out her own phone to see what everyone was talking about. Ross and Stuart joined me at the bar, their concerned faces mirroring my own and Tommy's.

The house lights went on and the music stopped. That scared me more than the alert message. For a sex club in the middle of Amsterdam, full of people to stop dead meant something was especially wrong. One of the hen's was crying jaggedly in the corner, attended to by her clucking consorts. The sound, along with the scraping of chairs and rapid-fire Dutch. was making me more and more anxious. Alcohol tinged sweat popped out on my back and armpits. The floor seemed to lurch a little. I wished I hadn't drunk quite so much as I had. My head was decidedly fuzzy.

"Get everyone here. We've got to get out of here and find out what's going on," I said to Tommy.

"Check out Captain Boy Scout. Coming to the rescue again eh? Jooo-NAH," laughed Ross.

"Oh. fuck off Ross," I tossed back over my shoulder as I made my way to the foyer. I could almost hear the spinning plates crashing to the floor around me.

Everyone seemed to be present when I arrived, standing in a little clump while the other customers pushed past them in the rush to get out of the building. The only person missing was Keith. John told me he was still upstairs with the strippers. Fighting the urge to scream and shake John for leaving yet another mess up to me to fix was an almost herculean effort. It was obvious I had been made the de facto parent, the only one able to corral man-babies through a crisis. To say I resented the role was an understatement. It would have been a relief for someone else to take it on for once, to gently take me by the elbow and show me the right way, eschewing the need for me to always be the responsible one. Looking around our little group, every man stared back at me with frightened, beseeching eyes. There was no choice, it was up to me.

Taking the stairs two at a time up to the striper's room, while dancers and customers alike fought against me like salmon in a fast moving stream, I had to resist the urge to shove. Fear makes for dangerous animals and it was imperative I stay calm or I'd sink to the floor and scream like a child having a tantrum or start swinging my fists. Action helped keep the panic at bay.

It was easy to spot Keith, sitting with a group of women on the plush sofas at one end of the room.

They were the only people not fleeing for their lives. A bottle of champagne sat gently sweating on the table in front of them.

"What the fuck are you doing?" I managed, breathlessly. The amount of booze, fried food and panic having made an impact on my fitness levels.

"Everyone is waiting downstairs for you. We gotta go see what's going on with this," I said, gesturing to my phone in my hand.

Keith's own phone was sitting on the table next to the nearly empty bottle of champagne. I couldn't see the screen but I bet it looked the same as mine; a terrifying alert message and no service.

"I'm not coming," Keith looked up at me belligerently, his meaty arm around two of the dancers who looked scared out of their wits, not least because of the tightness of Keith's grip.

"What do you mean you're not coming? Did you not see the alert?" I asked him, dumbfounded by his pugnaciousness.

"I did," Keith said sticking his chin up at me "and I'm not coming."

"I don't....you're not...WHAT?!" I asked him

angrily, unable to form into words how confused I was by his reticence to come with me.

"Joe. Look at me," Keith said, gesturing down to his formidable belly straining against his shirt. It was tumorous in its protuberance, hard like it should be holding a baby rather than a lifetime of beer and kebabs.

"I'm not like the rest of you. You're all fit, running around the pitch every week. I'm in goal because I'm scared the exercise is going to give me a heart attack," his eyes slid away from me in shame.

"If something really bad is going on, if you're all going to be running away from something, Martian invaders or nukes or something, then I'm just not going to be able to manage it," he shook his head sadly. "I just don't have the cardio. If I have to run for my life I'd be better off just lying down in the street to die, save myself the trouble. If this is the end of the world, then me and the girls are going to go out in style," he gestured to the bottle of champagne on the table "and if it's not you can just come back and get me later," he said shrugging.

"And they're OK with that?" I asked, gesturing to the small group of dancers left in the room. Some of them were sniffling away tears.

"We're as safe in here as anywhere else," Keith said, his broad shoulders falling in a defeated shrug. "They've said they're going to lock the doors once everyone leaves."

"You're sure?" I asked the assembled dancers.

"Ja, hoor," the woman sitting on the right of Keith said. She nodded her head a little in case I hadn't inferred the meaning.

I didn't want to leave him but other than picking him up and attempting the stairs in a fireman's lift there wasn't a lot to be done. I was also acutely aware the others were waiting for me downstairs and I now had a duty to them too. It didn't stop me turning around at the top of the stairs to take one last look at the most depressing looking sex show the world had ever seen; one stubborn fat man and a group of weeping strippers.

Returning to the foyer, I saw that Ross was breaking apart a small brown block and sharing it out around the group. He didn't look at me as I joined and I didn't really care. Stuart broke apart his section and handed it over to me.

"Brownie?" He asked before stuffing his share into his mouth.

"You're not serious are you?" I asked incredulously, the brownie smearing chocolate into my palm and tumbling crumbs onto the carpet. I could see Ross's grin as he looked at the floor. "Where did you get a brownie from?" I asked Stuart.

"Picked 'em up earlier," he said, gesturing to the open door that the last dregs of the customers were leaving from.

He pulled another out of his pocket, the packaging making a crinkling sound as he held it up. Not just a brownie but a "special" brownie. The last thing I wanted right then was to be in the middle of a potential disaster and stoned off my tits. I plonked the chocolaty mess back in Stuart's hand and made my way to the exit.

**

I feel sick as we take our seats in the auditorium, clammy and nauseated, like I'm trying to fight off a bad case of flu. My heart is galloping in my chest. I haven't been in any enclosed spaces in so long; no lifts, no cinema, no theatre or restaurants. I just can't be anywhere dark and contained where I could be trapped. I've barely left the house at all. Just to work and the supermarket. The wide, bright aisles of the supermarket are oddly comforting. Amelia isn't quite sure why I have taken on all of the shopping but she certainly isn't complaining. At home, I now insist on leaving the hall light on when we go to bed, leaving a sliver of light permeating the bedroom. At first I was embarrassed, like a kid needing a night light. But as an adult I have seen actual monsters and they're so much worse than the boogeyman under the bed. In my mind, it justifies the need for a little more light. A little more comfort.

Taking on all of the grocery shopping, and insisting on a night light are not the only changes to our household habits. Pre-Amsterdam (the way I now described my life, either pre or post) I had been a massive movie fan. I had a membership at the local cinema and always looked forward to the monthly newsletters, scouring the listings for something I just had to see. Sometimes, Amelia and I would splash out on the premium tickets; the roped off area at the back of the cinema with the plushy sofa-like seats. We'd snuggle up together with our array of snacks, probably spending more than if we'd gone out for dinner. I was a sucker for a Slushie, even if it did sometimes give me brain freeze. When my insecurities were in check, when I was healthy and happy, then a splurge on sweet popcorn and even sweeter iced drinks in front of the latest blockbuster with Amelia was my happy place.

A few months after my return, Amelia booked tickets to the cinema. She chose a comedy, realising there was no way I would be able to watch anything remotely scary or jumpy on a screen several feet high and in surround sound. Every little sounds around the house now made me jump and I couldn't abide anything loud or containing any strife on the TV. Any kind of tension, or the sounds of people arguing, had me instantly changing the channel. As the clock ticked round to the time we needed to leave, I became more and more nervous.

As I'd come out of the bathroom following the third or fourth emergency expulsion, well after the time we needed to leave, I saw Amelia sitting in the living room. The lights were dimmed but not off and a bowl of microwave popcorn sat on the coffee table. She patted the seat next to her on the sofa and pressed play on the DVD remote. It was one of my favourites, something I had seen a dozen times. I knew it so well I knew there would be nothing to shock me. The familiarity of it was comforting. For ninety minutes things almost felt like normal, like they had been before.

I could chicken out of going back to the cinema,

in the grand scheme of things it's not that important, but I can't chicken out of this. So, I've been gearing myself up for it all day, trying to find a work around to counter the almost debilitating dread that I woke with.

This morning I'd gone to the corner shop and bought a small bottle of their cheapest, nastiest own brand whiskey. I poured the majority of it into a half empty bottle of coke, just like I used to as a teenager to avoid detection on public transport on the way to a party or gig. The rest of it I decanted neat into a silver flask that Amelia bought me a few years ago for my birthday. I've been sipping at the bottle for most of the day, trying to keep the anxiety at bay. The flask went into the inside pocket of my jacket for the theatre. The weight of it against my chest is comforting, like a talisman. I take it out now and take a pull. The whiskey is not good, it is so harsh that it burns a comet all the way from my mouth to my belly but it gives me something to concentrate on and helps to stop the jittering of my restless legs. The bank of seats we're sitting on are locked in together and my constant movement is garnering some pretty poisonous looks from the couple at the end of the row. I doff the flask towards them before taking another, more measured sip. They turn away from me tutting and I cross my eyes at them childishly. Amelia looks at me with a comical face of disapproval. I'm not sure how much of it is gentle mockery and how much is real displeasure at my passive aggression. Either way she's trying to be especially gentle with me because of where we are. I don't know if that makes me feel better or worse.

Before I can put the flask back in my pocket, Amelia's hot hand is in mine. She slips the flask from me and takes a big slug. I try not to laugh at her face grimacing at the less than potable flavour of corner shop brand gut rot. She wipes the back of her hand across her mouth inelegantly and passes it back, her mouth turning down as she tries to smile at me. I have been so wrapped up in my thoughts about tonight that I haven't stopped to think how this might be making her feel. I know she has been trying to get me to open up about what happened but sitting in a theatre with a bunch of strangers hearing the nitty gritty details from someone that isn't trying to spare her feelings, is something else entirely. Neither of us know what this talk was really going to entail and how it is going to make us both feel. I take her hand and kiss the back of it, tasting the ghost of the whiskey on her skin. Her presence makes me brave and guilty that I have been less than totally honest with her. I scramble my brain for the right words to tell her how I really know Jennifer; not from an advert for her talk but as someone I'd stood beside as I watched people die. The words still elude me as the lights of the auditorium go down. It's too late. I grip her hand and suck in a big breath. She holds mine just as tight. Here we go.

The house lights come fully down and I try not to hyperventilate. My breath is hot, wet and fast in the gloom. I try to slow it down, sucking the air over my teeth and blowing it out again like I were at a Lamaze class. The darkness is oppressive and ominous, like having a thick blanket thrown over my head. I want to thrash to get it off me. The relief as the lights come back up quietens the tremoring of my body. Looking around it seems as thought I was not the only one to feel the reprieve of the lights. The auditorium is full of the sounds of people spared from what is now, for most of us, a torment. I look over at Amelia who also looks pained. Raising my eyebrows at her questioningly she smiles, pulling my clammy hand away from hers with a wet fart sound any Foley artist would be proud of. She gestures at the row of crescent moons I've left in her flesh when I clamped her hand in mine as the lights went down. I rub at them, whispering apologies to her. She shakes her head at me and rubs at the angry moons distractedly. Not knowing what to do with them, I sit on my hands and focus on the stage.

Jennifer looks different - confident and composed, her hair is sleek and her suit well fitting.

She looks nothing like the woman I met in Amsterdam. As she clicks the first slide into place I stare in horror at Jennifer's photo on the screen. Somewhere there is a photo of me much like this one. We all had our pictures taken when we arrived at the airport, before the debriefing. The woman on the screen, jubilant and bloody, is the woman I knew. The juxtaposition of the two women next to each other, one from the past, one in the present, gives me a horrible jolt. I barely listen to her explanations over the first couple of slides. I can only hear the pounding of my own heartbeat in my ears and the screams of the past. I close my eyes. I remember.

CHAPTER NINE: JENNIFER

I liked to think of myself as a smart person. I did alright at Uni, scraping past with a respectable 2:1. I read several daily newspapers to avoid bias and I always checked my facts first before posting online to avoid spreading disinformation. I thought I had critical, logical, problem solving skills as a reasonably competent adult. However, when faced with the choice of the stampeding crowd or being ripped limb from limb by salivating creatures, it was purely my reptile brain that took over, all self preservation and no higher cognitive function. I knew I couldn't run. I had been bottom of the class in PE at school and hadn't seen the inside of a gym in years. I didn't take the stairs, whether at work or up to my flat. Like a pursued fox I knew speed alone wouldn't save me and instead I had to decide whether to zig or zag to save myself.

There were already several bodies on the street around me. Like that fox, I had to swiftly find a burrow to escape into and hope the threat would run past me. Limping as swiftly as possible over to the shop fronts that ran alongside the road, I pulled on the first door and found it locked. The second was the same. By the third the roar of the crowd was increasing; swarming around my bruised, panicked body. I didn't bother to try the fourth and instead hit the glass of the door with the heels of both damaged hands, using so much force that my hand punctured the glass. Sharp shards stuck mercilessly into my flesh, but I couldn't feel it. Not yet. Adrenaline was saving me from that particular sensation for the time being. Shoving my bleeding appendage through the gap in the glass, I fumbled for the lock on the other side, making it slick and slippery with my blood. It wouldn't open. My fingers were clumsy and numb. Whimpering in panic, I leant my entire weight on the weak spot I'd made in the glass and heard it crack into rapidly splintering spiderwebs. I knocked at the cracks with my shoulder, my elbow and my poor minced hands. The glass splintered from the frame, raining down like confetti into my hair, over my face, down the back of my collar before smashing into the floor. I managed to force my way painfully through the small gap, wiggling my body against the sharp shards.

My final lunge sent me to my knees in the puddle of glass on the floor. But I was in. The heady, sweaty feet, podiatry stink of a room full of cheese hit me squarely in the face before a booted foot hit me full in the stomach. I hadn't seen anyone else in the shop, being far too focused at getting in. A surprised "oof" pushed out of me as I rolled across the floor. I looked up at the owner of the boot which had punted me across the vinyl floor, through the shards of broken glass. As he drew back his foot again, I crossed my arms instinctively over my face and heard another voice from somewhere deep in the shop shout out.

"What the fuck are you doing?"

"It's one of them!" the potential striker cried out.

I managed to roll onto my knees, trying not to retch onto a floor streaked and daubed with muddy footprints, crunching glass and the smears of my own blood. My hand came up instinctively, trying to ward the man off until I could summon enough breath to speak.

"I'm clearly a human being, you absolute melt," I managed to huff out painfully, forehead against the blessedly cool floor.

"Oh," came from above me.

There were many, many sarcastic rebuttals in my head. Many of them involving a lot of swearing, but I didn't have a chance to respond. A hand gripped my upper arm, and even though I was getting mighty sick of being manhandled at this point, I didn't seem to have an awful lot of breath left to complain, so instead I gulped uselessly at the air while the shop whizzed past. Other than winding me, the kick hadn't seemed to have done much damage. It was the only time I'd been kind of glad of additional padding to absorb the force. The arm pulled me along the floor, my shoes skidding and grappling, trying to find purchase amongst the broken glass. Finally, coming to a stop behind the counter at the end of the shop floor I came face to face with all the little knick knacks shop-keepers keep behind their tills; staplers, rubber band balls, business cards, carrier bags and a floor that could have done with a mop even before I arrived with my hands and knees dripping blood.

The man who had dragged me slumped down next to me, breathing hard. He was ashen, his eyes standing out starkly above high cheek bones. On the other side of me sat another man, his arms clasping his knees, rocking gently. He smelt like damp laundry, somehow sweet and foetid at the same time. It was how I imagined a carpet in a bathroom smells if you get right down close to it. I wondered absently if he always smelt like that or if it was a fear response. The all encompassing stink of the cheese, damp laundry man and the hefty kick to my mid-section was making me decidedly queasy. I stuck my head between my knees and tried to breathe through my nose.

"You OK?" the guy on my right asked me.

"Peachy," I managed, raising my thumb and forefinger in an OK sign without looking at him, huffing up all the air between my knees.

A bottle of water appeared under my nose and I took it gratefully, trying not to slug down the water too fast for fear it might make a hasty reappearance. It helped. Enough to allow me to look up again at the person who had offered it.

**

This is really where my story begins. I made it off the street and into relative safety, if you discount the kicking and the lacerated hands. I could have died on the street like so many people did. There is a lot of survivor's guilt in making it out alive but it didn't happen in a vacuum. There were other survivor's that helped me and I realise while speaking that as well as my own story, which I didn't think I would ever be recounting, especially in this manner, I am telling their stories as well. I don't know if that is OK or if I have the right to do so but it's too late. As Magnus Magnusson used to say during Mastermind "I've started so I'll finish."

I wish getting into the cheese shop had been the

end of my story. I wish I were standing here and saying "We stayed in that shop until we were rescued, ate tonnes of cheese and everyone lived happily ever after." I'd give anything for that to be true. But it isn't. If it were I wonder how much easier my life would be right now, whether I'd be so crippled by PTSD and regret. It's not healthy to dwell on it. It wasn't the end, it was only the beginning.

CHAPTER TEN: JONAH

My head was nearly taken off at the shoulders as I poked it out of the front door. The tight street was heaving with people. Even the women in the windows were pressed against the glass, trying to see what was going on. I could hear a swell of building noise somewhere close by. It reminded me of the slow rising clamour that happens before a concert, when people are waiting for their favourite artist to arrive on stage. That slow murmur builds and builds to thunderous applause, a charge that hung in the air. I could feel that charge now, but instead of it eliciting nervous excitement like at a gig, this charge was filling me with the static electricity feeling of panic. I would have given anything to just have the bass drop and have the tension dissipate in a room full of wild dancing, rather than be a part of this scrum on these cobbled streets.

"Excuse m..." I tried to the first person who walked past me. "Sorry could you...." I attempted with the next person. Maybe some actual Dutch would work. "Excuseer?" I said to the next person hurrying past me. The fourth I stood in front of, holding up my hand. "Hey!" I said a bit more forcefully than I meant to. "I'm sorry, could you tell me what's going on?" I asked the flustered looking woman who was jerking around me, trying to see the commotion.

"Pleur op," the woman said in a tone I knew to be exasperation, even if I didn't understand the words themselves. She pushed me out of the way and kept making her way towards the commotion in the distance.

"You heard her Joe-Joe, Op, Op, Chop, Chop," Ross said beside me "Why don't we go have a toodle on down there and see what the drama is?" He rubbed his hands in delight.

It didn't surprise me. Ross was the type of person to slow down when driving past an accident, just so he could tell you in graphic detail about the smear of blood he saw on the tarmac. I opened my mouth to tell him we should find out what was going on first, that we weren't all there anyway, that they had to help me get Keith down from upstairs, but before I could, Ross had danced out of the building like a mad Pied Piper, followed by his band of merry, soon to be very stoned, men. They started making their way down the street, weaving their way in and out through the rapidly gathering crowd.

"What's wrong Joe-Joe? Ya scared?" Ross called back to me.

"Yes," I whispered to myself, and jogged after them, trying desperately to keep their bobbing heads in sight as they disappeared into the crowd. I didn't want to see what was happening, but I didn't want to be left behind.

We followed the crowd down small streets, carried along with them over bridges and canals, well and truly trapped in the snaking conga line with no end in sight. Somewhere I lost the boys, one minute they were in front of me and then suddenly they were gone. I whipped around, trying to catch a glimpse of a familiar face, feeling like a child lost in a supermarket. Tears were threatening to spill down my cheeks. On my third rotation I caught him; Tommy standing still and splay legged in front of a shop window. His hands flat on the glass.

"Oh my god Ross I'm so HUNGRY!" he shouted, the inebriate's curse of thinking everyone else was deaf.

I cringed in embarrassment. A little voice wanted to yell "INSIDE VOICE!" at him like an exasperated school teacher. Just in time I realised the irony of, firstly, bellowing it at someone at all and secondly, howling it at someone while they were in-fact standing outside.

The edibles had obviously started to kick in and Tommy was locked in the grasp of the munchies. He was like a kid salivating outside a candy store, but this particular candy was wedged or wheeled and so strong I could smell it from outside the closed door. Ross was not so gently tugging on Tommy's sleeve, urging him to keep moving on a little more. I'm sure he was hoping to get to the action, which seemed to be gaining momentum at the canal's edge at the bottom of the street. Shouts and screams were mingling together in a symphony which was not helping the jangling of my nerves. This wasn't a long awaited concert, this was a lot more dangerous. I didn't want to go down to the canal.

Stuart and John were laughing about something I couldn't catch, leaning on each other and laughing helplessly. They wheezed and hitched, every time one of them tried to stand it would send the other into peels of laughter, doubling the first one over again in their mirth. Tim looked as though he was having an existential crisis; staring into the ether with a face that looked as though he'd just had an epiphany, or rather a reckoning. It was not a happy face.

I stood between Ross and Tommy, dropping a hand on both of their shoulders like a referee and tried to drop the annoyance from my voice.

"Come on now guys," I said in a voice that was coming over as more chilling than comforting. I realised I sounded like my dad when he went all quiet and calm before losing his ever-loving shit at me or my brother.

"Why can't we do both eh? Ross, let Tommy have a look for a bit and then we can go down and see what's going on. Alright?" I had distinct flashbacks to my dad having the same kind of conversation with my brother and I, mainly when one of us was pitching a fit or unwilling to share a toy. I had a renewed sympathy for him in this moment as well as a sense of horror that I was gradually turning into him.

Ross looked at me with daggers in his eyes but I could see his quandary. He was the good time guy. He couldn't kick up a fuss, he didn't want to not be the fun one. He was quite happy for me to keep that mantel. So with a quick nod of his head he pushed the door open to the little cheese shop.

The smell hit me in the face like a baseball bat. Still, at least it did a lot to cover the smell of Tommy's damp clothes. There were a couple of people inside, huddled together and speaking in excited Dutch, looking at their phones. I gathered they had received the same notification as we had but beyond that I was stumped, not having a clue what they were saying but wondering if I could butt in to ask. Behind me I could hear Tommy fall on the plate of free samples like he hadn't seen food in a week. Ross was still standing at the door, craning his neck at the window attempting to see the source of the commotion at the end of the street. Stuart and John made their way languidly into the shop, walking like all of their bones had been removed, still snickering gently to each other and seemingly unaware of the tension in the air.

Making my way over to the group, I tried to catch the eye of, the shopkeeper, adorned in an apron with the shop's logo and name on the front. I attempted my best polite tourist face, hoping my beer breath, panic sweat and braying comrades didn't put him off too much.

"Excuseer?" I said, really getting my money's worth from the handful of words I'd picked up from the back of the guide book.

The shopkeeper turned to me and tutted loudly before rolling his eyes and returning to the furiously fast Dutch conversation with his two companions. Obviously the emergency alert had pushed customer service low down on his priorities, I thought petulantly.

"Look. Hey," I tried again. If he wasn't going to give a shit trying to be nice then neither was I.

"The shop is closing," he threw back at me over his shoulder, not even turning to look at me.

"Good job I don't want to buy any fucking cheese then isn't it?" I said to his back. The man sighed dramatically and turned to me.

"Well that's good because the fucking shop is closing isn't it?" he sighed, hands on his hips. "Maybe if you don't want to buy something you can ask your friend to stop eating all of the samples hmm?" he gestured at Tommy who was too busy shovelling smelly little morsels into his mouth to realise anyone was talking about him and that maybe ten pieces of cheese was more than a 'sample'.

The shopkeeper made his way to the door and flipped the sign to closed. Making his way outside, past Tim who was still staring into the distance, he shielded his eyes to better see what was going on at the bottom of the street.

"I just wanted to ask you about the message that everyone got," I said, following him to the front of the shop and showing him my now useless phone.

I was still waving the ineffectual brick at him when the screaming started. The crescendo of anticipated noise had finally hit. But the bass didn't drop. My heart, on the other hand, seemed to drop into my underwear. The screaming was not the kind you hear from a group of teenagers finally seeing their boy-band crush on stage. It was horror movie screaming. It made every hair on my body stand up and pimpled every inch of flesh.

The little knot of Dutch customers joined the owner in the street to see what the commotion was. I didn't join them. Instead gesturing wildly at Tim to come into the shop I backed away from the window. He wandered in, still looking as though he was seeing through the dimensions of space and time. Thankfully he still had some presence of thought, or maybe it was just muscle memory, to close the door of the shop behind him. He hadn't got but two steps in when the first smatterings of the running crowd passed the shop window. It didn't look like a fun run or a marathon, it looked like people running for their lives.

When I saw what they were running from, I blew out a sigh of relief. They were just extras for a horror movie. Nothing to worry about. It was too far outside of the realms of possibility to be real. It was simply fake blood and prosthetics that made the staggering marauders look so real. We'd watch the film on Netflix in a few months time and point to the screen, saying with a smile "We were there! Look, that's the shop we were in, Tommy had the munchies for cheese!" Then I'd be able to tell the story about how Keith was happier to be left with strippers than come with us. How we'd gone back a couple of hours later to find him on the verge of debt and wearing a string of thongs like a necklace. It would all be a great big laugh. The smile died on my face when one of those horror movie extras, clothes ripped and dripping with canal water, sank its teeth straight into the meaty forearm of the shopkeeper.

I'd once read that the bite force of a human was around seventy pounds per square inch and for some reason that fact had lodged somewhere in the back of my brain. The person I'd thought was a horror movie extra, seemed to use every pound of that force as they bit down. It's teeth sank further and further into the shopkeeper's arm as he screamed and thrashed. His attacker seemed to be chewing as he grappled and snapped. Lumps of half masticated meat came flying out of his mouth to streak the front of his torn t-shirt and the cobbles below. Finally the shopkeeper lost his footing and his assailant jumped on him in a frenzy. I didn't see what happened next as the street darkened with the fleeing crowd and they vanished in the scrum.

"LOCK IT!" I shouted to Tim, who was gawping out of the glass window at the fleeing crowd. Amongst them were the creatures I'd dismissed as actors, like a pack of hyenas hunting within a stampede. Closer up it was ludicrous to think these things were anything other than creatures – humans didn't rip into other humans like this. Unless, of course, a hefty amount of bath salts had been consumed first. The sight of it seemed to have woken Tim out of his reverie and he pushed the lock into place. Grabbing onto his and Stuart's sleeves, I pulled them behind the counter and yelled for the others to follow. We hunkered down behind the wood, listening to the screaming on the street outside. It kept getting louder and louder like a train going through a station, just metres from where we all sat. I was more than a little aware that only a locked door and a thin piece of glass were protecting us from the carnage occurring on the street. Next to me Tim was muttering whatever he remembered of the prayers he'd been taught at school. On the other side of me Ross was reciting something under his breath too. Nothing as pious as Tim. It seemed to be every swear word he had ever learnt, some traditional and others mash-ups I had never heard before. Stuart's hand snuck into mine and I held on hard to it.

When the banging on the window began his grip

crunched the bones of my hand together painfully. I felt so dizzy with panic that my head didn't seem to be attached to my shoulders any longer. I just about managed to raise it enough to see over the counter, half expecting it to go floating off like an untethered balloon. I felt like a soldier sticking my head over the top of a trench and I hoped when my eyes opened that I death wouldn't be staring back at me. On the other side was a woman, two bloody hand prints smeared the glass in front of her. I had no idea whether she was one of those things or if she was someone running from them. When her second strike created a crack in the glass, I began looking around frantically for something to defend us. There were no suitable looking weapons in sight. The only choice seemed to be to throw a lot of cheese and hope it wasn't just flesh it wanted. Maybe the creatures were omnivores and would be satiated by a mature Edam rather than with my throat.

I ducked back under the counter to tell the others what I had seen but before I could get the words out Ross was up and out, walking stiffly on jerky legs. He stood beside the door, hidden from view by the window display. I watched as the woman wormed herself through the glass, straining and bleeding like some kind of abominable birth. Ross took a few steps back, pulling his leg back like he was kicking for the winning goal.

**

There it is. Jennifer describes making her way into that cheese shop and meeting a group of guys. It will soon become glaringly obvious that I am one of them. Amelia gasps next to me and coldness creeps over my entire body. She understands already. Now she knows why I booked the tickets for us to come here tonight. I don't have the words to explain to her everything that happened that weekend but Jennifer does. Through Jennifer's words she is going to hear everything. For better or for worse she'll know the truth. I am a coward who has left it up to this near stranger to explain everything to the love of my life, something that makes me ashamed and somehow relieved at the same time. The juxtaposition of two feelings sitting heavy in my breast is not new. It's the way I've felt every day since Jennifer broke her way through the glass of that cheese shop door. I am both lucky and cursed. It is a multiple personality feeling; the blessing of still being alive and the guilt of it. Both feelings vying to be in control of my body.

Amelia raises her hand and I expect to feel the sting of her palm against my cheek. Instead her cold fingertip wipes away tears that I didn't even realise were there. The tenderness of it is nearly my undoing. I expected her to be angry that I'd blind-sided her with this. But she seems to understand this is the only way I can give her the answers that she needs. She looks into my face and nods gently, wiping away more tears with the flat of her hands. I just hope after she hears everything she can still look at me like this and that when I look at her again she can bear to meet my eyes.

CHAPTER ELEVEN: JENNIFER

The man who had dragged me behind the counter and was now sitting next to me, offered me his hand, a touchingly formal gesture and introduced himself as Joe. Squinting at him with my puffy eye, I wondered if he was taking the piss but his face looked genuine. It was obviously now the time for official introductions. I showed him my own hands, bleeding and peppered with grit from my various falls. Understandably he didn't take one.

"Jennifer," I told him, tucking my damaged hands into my lap. He nodded grimly.

"That's Ross," he pointed to the kicker, who gave me a sheepish, tight-lipped smile. He gestured to the small huddle of men also sitting on the floor behind the counter. "This is Tommy, Stuart, Tim, John and er.. well just John I guess."

"I'd say nice to meet you, but...." I croaked, not finishing the sentence. Everyone knew there was nothing nice about this encounter. "Anyone know what the hell is going on?" I asked the assembled men. Each one stared back at me, mouths firmly closed. Shit. They were in the dark as much as me.

Joe began to rummage in a backpack at his feet, from where I assumed the previously proffered bottle of water had come from. He passed me a box of plasters, a roll of sweets and some paracetamol. I took all of them gratefully and sucked down two paracetamol with a glug from the bottle of water. I doubted it would do much for the pain of my various bumps and cuts but maybe even a placebo effect would be helpful. The film on the packet of sweets was rolled back like a polo neck, so tight I had to tear it away with my fingernails. I noticed how ragged they were, many of them torn and sharp from my fall and fight with the glass door. Finally, managing to wrestle one free, I popped a bright pastel coloured sweet into my mouth. The flavour was almost overwhelming on the sour dryness of my tongue. It brought a tear to my eye and reminded me starkly of the owner of the coffee shop and his kindness to me the day before. I hoped he was OK. Apart from the hotel clerk who'd gone MIA and the distracted Uber driver, he was the only other person I'd had a friendly conversation with. I hoped he hadn't ventured out to see what the commotion was, and been dragged down into the silty depths of the canal by one of those – things. I badly wanted to go and see if he'd made it. What I wouldn't give to sit in his glass and flora ensconced space, a little oasis of calm, not in the cheesy old feet stench of this little shop with the cold December air whistling through the crack I'd made.

It wasn't a small hole. I'm not a small woman, and my worming through the gap had knocked out most of the glass.

Joe pulled down a roll of paper from above the counter, the shiny kind used to wrap cheese before handing it over to a customer. He carefully ripped a sheet from it and passed it to me, motioning silently at my bleeding hands. I held the non-porous paper to them. It smeared the blood but did nothing to soak it up. At least it made it a little easier to open the packet of plasters he'd offered me. How prepared was this guy? I hadn't even thought to bring my handbag from the hotel. All that was in my pockets were the hotel key, my useless phone and a tube of lip balm.

All of the plasters in the box were tiny, a travel sized box for travellers who'd bought new shoes for their trip and had a blister rather than someone who had turned their hands into useless, bloody slabs of meat. Also inside the box was a packet of alcohol wipes. It might have been suitable for a blister or a hangnail but rubbing alcohol on large open wounds is a staggeringly bad plan. I beat my feet on the floor from the burning, trying not to cry out and alert anyone or, more importantly, anything to our position. Biting my tongue so hard against the pain, the taste of fresh blood was hot in my mouth. I'd need a bloody transfusion after all this, I thought bitterly.

It took several minutes for the pain to abate enough to allow me to speak.

"Where are we?" I managed to huff out. Joe looked around the shelves of cheese. He seemed to be wondering whether or not to give me the flippant answer of "Well in a cheese shop obviously." He had the rare ability to seemingly wear all of his thoughts right out on his face. I think my expression made the decision for him. I was not in the mood for flippancy.

"We're on one of the nine streets. I don't know if it's Wolvenstraat or Hartenstraat though. I didn't catch the name as we came in here," he answered, peering out of the window. I didn't think the sliver of sky we could see from underneath the counter was going to help him but I bit my sore, bleeding tongue. My own flippancy would surely not be appreciated either.

I'd read about the nine streets during my snatches of lunchtime research, sitting at my desk dropping crumbs between the letters of my keyboard. It was lauded as one of the best places for shopping and part of the UNESCO Heritage site. I'd been planning on spending a day trawling cute, boutique shops and warming myself with crepes or pancakes in one of the cafes before visiting somewhere cultural. A shudder gripped me involuntarily – how much worse would this have been trapped in a gallery or a museum with nowhere to hide from the creatures? Suddenly I was very grateful for the hiding place I found myself in, even with the overwhelming smell of ripe cheese and the damp party boys crammed in next to me.

"We can't stay here," said Joe, gesturing to the door. There were a lot of accusatory eyes on me. I didn't meet any of them but nodded at him.

"I know somewhere we can go," I said.

Joe's face pinched in on himself as I told him and the rest of the group about the coffee shop owner from yesterday. It was so pinched that he resembled a wizened old apple by the end of my story. I could tell exactly how bad of a plan he thought my idea was. It was written large on his face. It couldn't have been clearer unless it was lit in neon.

"I don't really care whether or not you want to come with me. I'm going," I said, sticking my chin out and hoping it didn't wobble at all.

Not being a betting woman and hoped my poker face was good enough. I was no damsel in distress needing to be saved by a big strong man, but neither was I stupid enough to hamstring myself with my own ego to prove a point. If they all decided it really was a bloody awful plan I would acquiesce and stick with them. They might be a group who included a man who smelt very odd, and one whose first instinct was to kick first and ask questions later. But they at least spoke the same language as me. It was also better than being out there alone with people who might literally throw you to the wolves just to get hold of an already stolen bike.

The rest of the men huddled together to discuss the plan. Joe didn't join them. Instead he took a little hunk of particularly ripe smelling cheese from the counter above and shuffled himself to be more comfortable on the floor. He sat beside me taking small nips out of it like a cartoon mouse. I waved away the chunk he offered me.

"You not joining the committee?" I asked him, trying to breathe through my mouth. The smell was truly overwhelming.

"Nah. They don't really want my input. I'll just go along with whatever is decided. Story of my life Jen," he said, crumbling a cracker from a swiped packet into his lap.

"Jennifer," I corrected him automatically "Sorry, force of habit," I shrugged. I'd spent almost my entire adult life correcting people on the alternative pronunciations and spellings of my name.

"Sorry. Jennifer. " He smiled quickly, a bright flash of teeth in the only expression I'd seen from him that I could not quite fathom.

I watched the huddled group of men argue amongst themselves. It was the first time I realised they were all wearing themed shirts. Each of them seemed to have their name and 'Stu's stags" emblazoned on them. I couldn't see the back of Joe's shirt as he sat next to me on the floor but it was obviously fucking massive. Now their reason for being in Amsterdam was apparent. It wasn't the most auspicious start to married life and I wondered if Stuart The Stag was taking it as an omen.

As I mused waiting for them to come to a decision, I dug my phone out of my pocket, hoping my various falls hadn't smashed it to bits. The screen was a spiderweb of cracks, but it still worked. That pesky 'No Service' message was still at the top of the screen. Mocking me. I could only assume the hotel was not the problem and the whole city was out of service. Maybe it was too many people trying to call loved ones or visa versa. Maybe the Wi-Fi had been inundated with people hunkering down with a really banging Spotify apocalypse soundtrack. Whatever the reason for the outage it meant no online maps. It also meant I had become one of those annoying millennials who were scuppered because of their reliance on their phones. I hadn't bought a guide book with me and wouldn't even have considered buying a paper map. The last time I had seen one was in the rear seat pocket of my dad's car as a kid. I was literally adrift in a country I'd only been in a day, without a grasp of the language and with an internal compass which was spinning wildly.

"Fine. We'll go to this coffee-shop," Stuart The Stag said belligerently. The group had obviously come to a decision on the matter. "Where is it?" he asked me. My brain froze. I had no idea. I almost gasped when Joe pulled a battered looking map out of the back pocket of his jeans. It was as wondrous a sight as if he'd pulled out a Fabergé Egg.

"Captain Boy Scout to the rescue," he said sourly, flicking a loaded glance towards the man whose shirt said Ross but who I would always think of as The Kicker.

He smoothed the map out on the grubby floor between us. It wasn't the most detailed map, but I could work out where my hotel was, and then walk my finger down the roads until it landed on the site of the coffee-shop. It was just one street and one canal over from where we were currently huddled.

"Okay, it's literally only a couple hundred metres. We can go over there and if it's a blood bath then it's not far for us to get back here," Joe said. I quivered at his words. I didn't want to walk into another scene from a horror movie, I had seen enough bodies to last me a life time already.

"Do you think we should take supplies?" The Kicker asked wobbly, leaning over us. He reeked of booze and his eyes seemed to be too different sizes, not that either of them was able to focus on me. I was astounded he was still standing upright. I was surprised most of them were standing upright. Only Joe seemed to be in any way sober.

"For a couple of hundred metres? How long do you think it's going to take Lionel Messi?" I spat unkindly in his direction.

"The foot of God," he said taking a stumbling little bow which almost tipped him straight over.

"Wasn't meant as a compliment, genius," I huffed.

The fear over whether or not this was a ludicrous decision and the pain from my hands and eye was making me nasty. But, this twat had booted me in the stomach so I didn't feel that bad as his cheeks coloured. In honesty I was more than a little impressed that I had remembered the name of a footballer. It wasn't my forte but I'd once found myself watching an entire season of football in a short-lived relationship with a man who probably would have been happier to date an actual football than me. Something must have stuck in my brain from all those games I was forced to watch in the pub, a group of men roaring in my ear at every goal or near miss while I got steadily more and more drunk out of sheer boredom. I'd never eaten so many Scampi Fries in my life.

It was my fault that the shop was no longer secure and it was my suggestion on the next place to go so it only seemed fair for me to be the first one to actually physically leave. Knowing it was fair didn't make it any less terrifying. My joints were full of sand as I stood, rasping and sore. Tottering experimentally on legs burning with exhaustion, I left the den-like safety behind the counter. Struggling to the window, I peered around my own clammy, bloody handprint on the glass, onto the street.. The dried blood sigil seemed like a terrible portent of things to come. The street beyond was quiet, empty of living people but full of debris from the crowd and littered with the bodies of the dead. Some had been crushed by the force of the fleeing scrum, some had been torn apart by the creatures from the canal. The cobbles were daubed with their blood, great splashes of red against the stone and pooling in puddles in the gutters. The coppery tang of it seeped through the whistling hole in the door. Part of me still desperately hoped it was an elaborate piece of street art. Maybe I would take one step outside and all of the bodies would stand and cheer, pointing delightedly to hidden cameras and jolly TV hosts. My brain couldn't fully comprehend the horror painted onto the pavement outside or the stillness of bodies too badly damaged to be anything other than dead.

I opened the shattered remains of the glass door and stopped dead in my tracks. My bowels went cold as the little bell above it tinkled out melodically into the deathly silence. My head was full of visions of those things coming back, surging into the shop and tearing into us with their nails and teeth. It was probably only down to sheer dehydration that I didn't wet myself. Small mercies. Turning back, the knot of men in the shop were watching me with panicked faces. No-one else had moved from behind the counter. Joe stood with his hand over his heart, eyes closed. There was some relief that it wasn't just me that the bell had affected. It made me feel less of a coward to see my fear mirrored on their faces too. Not trusting myself to speak I gestured towards them with my hand, beckoning them to follow me.

**

*"Why didn't you stay where you were?"
someone shouts down from one of the higher seats.*

*I don't blame them for the question. I often ask
myself the very same one. It was true that my way
into the shop had made it insecure. But we probably
could have muddled through and botched a fix, had
we really thought hard about it. There was a
veritable treasure trove of stuff behind the counter
and the counter itself was heavy enough to have
acted like a barrier, had we thought to push it up
against the hole. There hasn't been a day since
where I don't wonder what would have happened if
we hadn't left the shop. Would we have hunkered
down, gorged on looted cheese and awaited rescue?
Would the shop have been over-run with the
creatures and we would have been just one of the
many names recorded on a memorial plaque in the
city? There's no way to know and you can drive
yourself insane with all of the possibilities. You
can't live in all of the alternate realities stretching
into infinity.*

*That's the problem with what-ifs, they're mainly
a thought experiment in decision making. I used to*

be great at decision making. The whole of my work day was a plethora of hard and fast selections and resolutions with barely a pause. And if something went wrong I would shrug and say "Well at least nobody died." But since returning from Amsterdam every decision that needs to be made is almost debilitating. I had witnessed first hand the fatal consequences of making the wrong one. Now the pressure of every one of them is in my head, giving me the bends.

Even though I didn't return to my marketing job I wasn't rich enough to give up work entirely. The bills still needed to be paid so I took a data entry job that could be done from home. It pays a fraction of my old one but it's a respite from decision making, with the added bonus of not having to mix with anyone and cover up the fact that I am broken in a fundamental way. Every day is a fight to keep my head above water. I don't have the mental capacity to care about a whip-round for Carol's birthday or the drama of who is shagging who. Instead I sit alone, with the TV on low and input data all day. It's incredibly boring but it helps to focus on something else for a few hours and it's a monthly salary that just about pays for my astronomical lighting bills and a weekly takeaway. I can no longer stomach the smell of cheese on a pizza but I'm the Chinese takeaways new best customer.

Even though I no longer have the capacity to engage in office gossip or politics it doesn't mean I'm not really incredibly lonely at home all day by myself. I thought about dating; meeting someone new who doesn't know anything about me. A completely new slate. I downloaded Tinder but become stuck at the first couple of profiles – swiping one way could obliterate the possibility of my soulmate but swiping the other might mean dating a man who ruins my life? Do I put on there that I can no longer eat cheese because the smell is synonymous with death? Or that I can't sleep in the dark? Even choosing a therapist to help me deal with my crippling anxiety around decision making has been beyond me. I realise the irony of it but it doesn't make it any easier. It took me a month to decide to take this speaking opportunity. Looking out onto the crowd of faces I still don't know if it was the right decision or not.

"What would you have done?" I ask him.

He gawps at me, mouth opening and closing like a fish. I can almost hear the cogs turning from here. It's not such an easy decision when it's your skin on the line, when it goes from thought experiment to survival. I'm alive. Others were not so lucky.

CHAPTER TWELVE: JONAH

I'd told Jennifer that there was no point joining the decision making huddle because no-one would listen to me. While that was partially correct, it was also because I had no idea which course of action was best. We couldn't stay in the shop, that much was clear. The hole in the glass stared at me, like a bright white eye, making me feel exposed and vulnerable but Jennifer's coffee-shop plan did not make me feel any better. The thought of leaving the, relative (seeing as we hadn't yet been attacked) safety of the shop to go into the unknown made my mouth go dry. There was no doubt that we were monumentally lucky to have been in a place of safety when the creatures had rushed through the street, killing everyone unable to flee. The thought of pushing that luck was not particularly appealing but I wasn't sure which plan did so. Maybe both. The conflict was making me sweat under the giant sail of my stag do shirt. I had no definitive answers to give.

My uncertainty was quelled a little when Jennifer raised her chin and told us she was going whether or not we came too. I admired her confidence and unwavering strength of her conviction. Finally, maybe I'd found the other adult that I'd been searching for, someone to share the burden of stag do childcare with. It made my decision to follow her an easy one which was a relief. That sense of relief wavered somewhat when the shop bell tinkled in the silent air, alerting anyone who might have been in range to our presence. It departed entirely when I walked out onto the street. There were no good feelings to be found here. This was not the street I'd walked down less than hour ago, this was a street from a war zone. It more closely resembled somewhere I'd only ever seen on the news, sitting safe and warm in my living room impatiently waiting for the football scores to come on. Not that I was completely lacking in empathy. I'd donated to chuggers in the street, clad in bright shirts with 'Save the' emboldened across them, rattling their tins for those in war torn countries or victims of natural disasters. I felt good about myself when the coin hit the bottom of the can and then thought no more about it for the rest of the day. It had seemed unfathomable that one day it could be me standing on a desolate street wondering how to pick my way across puddles of blood and bodies. It was impossible to be detached about this. It was in front of me. I could see and smell it. I was a part of it.

I tried to regulate my breathing, trying to stop it becoming a desperate pant of panic as my toe nudged a lifeless and unyielding body. It might have been the remnants of the shopkeeper or any of the customers who'd gone out with him. It might have been a stranger from the crowd. It was impossible to tell from the little that was left of their face. It seemed unfathomable that this lump of meat, which resembled something from an abattoir, was once a living, breathing human being only an hour beforehand. Logically I knew no-one could survive such injuries, in the rational part of my brain. The illogical part, which had watched too many horror movies, was convinced the corpse was most definitely going to shoot out a dead hand to encircle my ankle in an iron grip and pull me into its murderous embrace. I had to cram my knuckles into my mouth to stop the scream that leapt up my throat when Tim came up behind me, grabbing onto the sleeve of my jacket like a child trying to get my attention. I bit into the bony knobbles hard enough to taste my own blood on my tongue. With the other hand I grabbed onto Tim and we helped each other over the mound of bodies. I was glad of the warmth of his hand amidst all the frigid death around us. I didn't bother looking behind me, just kept stepping on and on, hoping the carpet of corpses would end soon. There didn't seem to be an end in sight.

It is an odd feeling to hear your own lived experiences told from the perspective of another. Jennifer describes meeting me and my actions leading up to leaving the cheese shop. I'm both fascinated and incredibly self conscious at the same time. My mum always used to tell me not to linger at doors, because you might not like what you'd hear. She'd often find my brother and I trying to garner any snippet of valuable adult information. We'd sit on the top of the stairs when we should be in bed, listening to the adults talking about us in the warm kitchen. She was right. We sometimes didn't like what we heard. It didn't stop us from quietly sneaking into place, night after night. Even if our feelings got hurt. The thrill of hearing adults talk about us was too heady a drug to easily give up.

I could let Jennifer know that I am here. But, as uncomfortable as it is, it is also riveting to see what she is going to say about me. It's the effects of that old drug all over again. As an adult, now very aware of their own mortality it is less the thrill of thinking you are important to an adult and more like listening in at your own eulogy. You're hoping someone is going to say something nice about you, but you also know you're not actually dead and you don't know when is the right time to pop up from your pine box to scare the shit out of the mourners. A jack-in-the-box cadaver. It's an unreal feeling. The Joe she describes could be a character in a book. It could be that the familiarity I am experiencing is because I've read the book before, not because they are my memories. I know the character didn't get involved in the initial decision making before they leave, because Jennifer tells us. But I also know that he was revolted every time his shoe found purchase on something that was not pavement after they left, something that Jennifer could not know. But surely the grotesque squishing sound in my head is just the result of my powerful imagination, not my memory? It's just down to Jennifer's storytelling skills, isn't it? I wonder if anyone here pities the plight of poor Joe. They are just an audience to someone else's misfortune, much like when I used to sit in my living room and watch the news, sombrely shaking my head but forgetting all about it when the scores came on. It's something that happens to other people, all very sad but ultimately forgotten when you go about your own life. Right?

I could leave now and get back to my own life. I could let Jennifer narrate me to a bunch of strangers and not care about it, leave it all behind in this once opulent theatre. Yes that's what I'm going to do. But my legs don't move. Glaring down at them, I am furious to be betrayed by their inaction. Just like sitting on the top of the stairs with my brother, I knew I should go back to bed, knew that I would be exhausted at school tomorrow. But the anticipation of hearing something important kept me rooted to the spot, making my bum go numb on the thin carpet of the top step.

Looking over to Amelia, I hope that I've somehow telepathically communicated my desire to leave to her. I hope that she is going to lean over and whisper in my ear that if we leave now we'll get back in time before the chippy near the station closes and we can walk home with a steaming bag of hot, vinegary chips and forget any of this ever happened. It's not to be. Amelia is engrossed, leaning forward in her seat, ravenous for the details of what happened. Her hunger for the minutiae knocks me off balance. I feel incredibly vulnerable, like the flesh is being picked from my bones by this ravenous crowd, gobbling down my life experiences with both hands. I don't like it. Not one little bit.

CHAPTER THIRTEEN: JENNIFER

There were so many bodies on the street. If only I could have closed my eyes, saved myself from having to see the damage done to them right there and again in the future. But the carpet of corpses was so dense that there was no choice but to carefully look to avoid stepping or tripping on any of them, injuring myself more than I already was. I shuffled past a woman who had obviously been on her way home from the supermarket. She lay next to her blue Albert Heijn shopping bags, which had spilled all of their contents out onto the pavement - a lettuce starting to curl, a crushed bag of fruit, everyday groceries left to spoil next to the rapidly cooling puddle of blood that had seeped from their former owner. Her glassy, gelatinous eye looked up at me in an accusatory manner, furious that her groceries were spoiling in the afternoon air. Didn't I know she was going to have to go back and buy everything again, there was nothing for dinner and the kids would be home soon? I shuddered. She could have been someone I'd jostled against as I'd run from the creatures. Had I veered left instead of right, if I'd been on foot rather than on that stolen bike, then that could have been me lying there instead. She could have been with this group of men and looking down at me as they fled the scene to safety. The thought made me feel vertiginous, like I was looking out of both her dead gaze and my own living sight. Leaning down to put my hands on my knees, hoping the world would stop spinning, I breathed the smell of death deep into my lungs. It was coppery like the tang of a butcher's shop, coating the back of my throat. I struggled not to retch, desperate to not make more sound than absolutely necessary.

The rest of the group had passed me as I grappled with my nausea and were making their way down the road, picking their way gingerly amongst the piles of the dead. I watched them go and felt tired, tired down to my very marrow, not all together confident that I had the strength to continue. What if I lay down next to this woman, my death doppelgänger, my cold counterpart and went to sleep on the frigid cobblestones? Then there would be no further decisions and no having to face the consequences of the ones already made. I considered it and might well have done it if one of the men had not yelled at me to hurry up. I know it was everybody's very first apocalypse but surely common sense would tell you that yelling while you were trying to make a silent get away, was a spectacularly bad plan. Undeniably this guy was lacking something in the sense department. I squinted to see who it was. The Kicker. Obviously.

The city of Amsterdam is laid out a bit like a spiderweb, with concentric canals linking the streets. The nine streets or De 9 Straatjes, where we found ourselves are long and narrow, lined with shops and cafe's. The streets ended in canals before continuing onward. There were very few places to dodge into or hide, the only way out was forward and fast. I started to run. The eerie silence of the street was soon broken by pounding footsteps and guttural snarling. I didn't turn to look back and see what was making the noise. I'd screamed at enough movies to know a woman looking behind her while running was bound to trip on something, even something invisible and go sprawling to the floor, letting her attacker easily catch up and fall on her prone body to enact their murderous desires. There were enough trip hazards for me to go down while looking where I was going, let alone if I started running blind. The sound of the creatures, shrieking and howling, their feet hitting the cobblestones behind me, where I couldn't see, was torturous. It was an avalanche of sound rushing up behind me and threatening to engulf me in sharp teeth and tearing hands. The air burned in my lungs as I pumped my arms, urging my tubby body forward. The cold wind whipped the salty tears out of my one good eye. My limbs began to burn, filling quickly with lactic acid.

"Oh shit. Oh shit. Oh shit," I puffed out with

every breath.

I had already been way behind the group of men before they'd started running, but I was falling further and further behind with every gasping step. Soon they would reach the end of the road and I would be on my own. No-one was going to risk their own neck to come back and help me out. Why would they? They barely knew me, and in the little time they had, I'd put them in danger. Twice. Coming back for me was suicide. I really, really didn't want to die but I didn't know how much more running I was capable of. Cardio had never been my strong point. I avoided it as much as possible. I'd once gotten off the tube at Camden town and seeing that the lift was out of order and the only way out was the ninety-six steps of the spiral staircase, gotten back on the train. Suffice to say exercise was not my drug of choice, ice-cream was. However, like any addiction, the effects of this drug were now very much to my detriment. A stitch gripped painfully at my side, almost as sharp as the teeth that I was running from.

Wiping my sleeve across my face, trying to stop the streaming liquid blinding me more than I already was took only a second but when I cracked open my good eye, the rest of the group had disappeared from view. Horror stricken, I whipped my head around to see them. They were nowhere to be found. I was totally on my own and the creatures were gaining on me. I was the weak gazelle that had been left behind by the rest of the herd to appease the advancing predators. That bunch of bastards! I screamed out in frustration, not caring if it was drawing the creatures to me. My death seemed inevitable at this point.

Out of the corner of my eye I could see one of the things coming up beside me, pumping arms hanging with tendrils of flesh, its face a ravaged mask of sinew, bone and teeth. So many teeth. Teeth waiting to sink into my skin and tear it away. As I ran closer to the buildings to avoid a cluster of bodies on the street, a hand grabbed on to the back of my top. I screamed louder and wrenched forward, trying to break free from its grasp. But it held tight and other hands joined it, pulling me in the same direction. I couldn't keep running. This was it. I was going to be slaughtered. My scream petered out into wrenching, wretched sobs.

"Stop fighting!" someone shouted in my ear.

I stopped struggling and twisted my head towards the voice in shock. It was a man, definitely a living human man leaning out of the shop doorway. Beside him were the other guys from my group. It had been their hands holding on to my shirt, trying to drag me in to safety, rather than drag me away to be eaten.

Relief made my whole body weak and I allowed myself to be pulled by the many hands through the open doorway, a dark maw on the dusky street. The door slammed closed behind me and the hollow bonk as the forehead of the creature hot on my heels met with its surface was loud in the small space. It had been so close behind me it had nearly gotten inside. There hadn't been had a second to spare.

Two men I didn't recognise passed a piece of wood to each other, sliding it into place behind the door. It looked like another door, taken off its hinges, and made into an impromptu barricade. Everyone present, apart from me, leaned against it. Thumps and bangs and scratches and squeals rained down on the wood like a meteor storm. The screams and roars of frustration from the creatures were booming in the dark vestibule. The assault was frenzied but short lived. It seemed as soon as the creatures could not see us any longer, then they stopped trying to get to us. Out of sight out of mind. Who knew the living dead would have such short attention spans?

Sitting on the sticky foyer floor I watched the barrier until the sounds beyond it dissipated, willing it to stay in place. I stared at the wood with such ferocity I thought my eyes might burn holes through it. When a hand fell on my shoulder again, wrenching me from my reverie, the noise I made was not dignified. It was somewhere between a squawk and a moan. The man who'd touched me jumped back like he'd been burned. The look on his face turned my moan into snotty, hiccuping giggles. The pressure valve release of relief was too much and I dissolved into wet, hitching guffaws, bloody hands on knees, tears squirting down my cheeks. I rolled onto my back, like a prone turtle, almost waterboarding myself with my own tears and snot. Eventually, the laughter burned itself out and I felt able to begin trying to stand. Rolling onto my shredded knees I pushed myself up like a toddler, palms flat against the floor until my legs were securely underneath me. They were wobbly from burned off adrenaline and an unheard of amount of exercise but they managed to take my weight. Swaying slightly I looked around.

"Alright?" Joe asked me from his place next to the door. The ghost of a smile played at the corners of his mouth.

"Oh yeah. Absolutely peachy mate," I said wiping the tears away from my face with the back of my hand and smiling ruefully back at him.

At his words everyone seemed to relax, no longer watching my tentative stand like a spectacle;

a baby giraffe taking its first steps at the zoo, who may or may not be about to fall spectacularly. There was a ripple of relieved laughter and manly back slapping as the group thanked our rescuers for letting us in. I grinned maniacally at both, trying to swallow the lump in my throat. There were no words for the gratitude that danced through my veins and I definitely didn't want to start crying again. I might have looked like someone who'd recently escaped a wood chipper and who had squawked like a shocked turkey but I still had some pride and crying twice in quick succession was beyond the pale.

The two men introduced themselves as Brad and Michael before leading us out of the entryway and up a steep staircase to a second room. The glowing neon sign above the stairs announced our sanctuary as a coffee-shop. It wasn't the one we were aiming for, but it was a coffee-shop just the same. As we walked into the second room, they closed the door to the stairs and pushed furniture up against it as a second blockade. I really hoped that this wasn't a belt and braces approach, that they weren't worried that the first barricade would fail.

This coffee-shop was very different to the first one I had been to. Whereas that one had been light and airy this was dark and cosy, with deep crimson velvet banquettes facing one another and thick

Persian-style rugs on the floor that seemed to have absorbed all the dense, sweet scent of marijuana. Low lights bounced off the painted black walls, giving the room the feel of a black box, like the drama studio we used to have at school. Apart from the boarded up door in the foyer there seemed to be no windows at all. It felt pretty secure. At least I hoped so.

Dotted around the room were more people, all in various stages of intoxication. Brad and Michael appeared to be the most sober and even they were a little glassy eyed. Curled into the fetal position, in what looked to be a state of catatonia, was a girl that her friend Kate introduced to us as Meg. They were American exchange students who'd been away from campus for the day. On the opposite banquette were three men, looking surprisingly relaxed. Charlie had his feet up on the detritus strewn table, the hem of his jeans soaking up the rapidly advancing spill of an overturned bottle. I watched a little river of juice and flecks of weed heading towards the lip of the table. Whatever didn't soak into the denim of his jeans dribbled noisily onto the carpet. It was oddly hypnotic. He looked like a man on holiday and not someone seeking shelter in what was rapidly starting to feel like the first hours of the end of the world. The man next to him, Jake, was skinning up with the fervour of a man clinging to a life raft. He pushed up his glasses every couple of seconds as they slipped down his sweaty nose. The third, Ian looked like he was trying to grab Kate's attention as she administered to her gently rocking friend. I wondered if he was going to try to encourage her to find solace in his embrace. Trauma bonding at its finest.

Michael made the introductions around the room and those already seated either smiled weakly, nodded, or in Meg's case failed to respond at all. Joe took the lead and introduced our little group. After the introductions were made nobody moved. It was like a school disco with kids standing on either sides of the gymnasium not knowing how to react. It was painfully awkward. I wasn't the only one to jump when Brad went behind the counter and began banging around, filling the expensive looking coffee maker with ground coffee. He turned the milk frother up to full blast and leaned over the counter towards me, a fat marker pen in his hand.

"Name?" he asked me, wiggling his eyebrows, hoping I'd get in on the joke.

"Jennifer," I rasped back at him. He plonked the plastic cup of steaming hot coffee in front of me. "Marnie" was hastily scrawled on the side in marker.

"Spot on," I said, taking the cup and cradling it

in my poor, cold, eviscerated hands. It hurt but the heat was worth it. A croak of laughter escaped through my chapped lips.

Brad asked every person their name and gave them each cups of hot coffee with sillier and sillier names penned on the side. It was the perfect ice-breaker.

Sitting heavily on one of the banquettes, seeing a little puff of dust shoot up around me, I sipped the coffee experimentally. It wasn't how I usually took it but it was hot and very sweet, exactly what was needed. The amount of running my poor battered body had done hit my system like a sledgehammer. Even the caffeine couldn't do much against the fatigue. My eye, still swollen closed, smarted from tears and sweat. All of my scraped and lacerated skin smarted and throbbed, especially that pressed against the hot cup. The urge to curl up on the seat like Meg and cry was strong.

Ross swaggered back from the counter, "Clarence" written across his cup. It wouldn't have been the name I'd have chosen for him but Brad was yet to find out what a bellend Ross was. He sat on the other side of the banquette from me and sighed dramatically, pulling his shirt up to mop his face, giving me an eyeful of his hairy, sweaty six pack. It seemed a very tried and tested move but in very poor taste given the circumstances. I rolled my eyes over the rim of my cup at Jonah. He spat out a mouthful of his own coffee and hid his snickering behind a volley of fake coughing. Ross didn't look pleased when the shirt came down from his face. He picked up his coffee cup and stalked to the other end of the room, dropping himself down to sit at the table with Charlie, Ian and Jake. They all gripped each other's hands manfully, nodding at each other, biceps flexing under their shirts. If my eyes had rolled back any further I would have done myself an injury. The amount of testosterone in the room was going to make me gag.

**

Talking about Brad and his coffee cups makes me realise that pseudonyms for the other people in this story might have been a good idea. Maybe I could have even used the same ones from those long ago coffee cups.

Reminiscing on that time is almost worse than remembering running for my life before it. There were moments, pockets of warm camaraderie between us before things got worse. There was a time when I thought we were going to be okay and I was full of relief at not being killed. Remembering

Brad wiggling his eyebrows at me and making silly puns is almost too hard to bear. I put my hand on my chest, feeling the weight of the memory trying to cleave me in two. I hadn't expected that. I thought I'd talk through some prepare slides, maybe answer some questions and then head back to the safety of my flat to drown myself in Pinot and ice-cream. I've gone off piste without thinking about the consequences. Again. I don't have their permission to be telling their stories like this and have no idea if they would be comfortable with my doing so.

Something is tugging at the back of my mind, a forgotten mantra, like a snatch of a jingle from an old show, waiting to fall off the tip of my tongue. As the memories of the others tumble into my mind I know that there is something I have forgotten but the connection is momentarily lost to me. It's too late. I can't stop here. As painful as it is I have to tell the end of the story. Not for me, but for the others. Telling their stories is the very least they deserve.

CHAPTER FOURTEEN: JONAH

The room quickly quietened down, like an engine ticking itself cool after a frenzied car chase. Danger was no longer an unsecure entrance, or something to flee from at top speed on the street. It was no longer pummelling on the door and trying to force itself inside. The giggling had been very near to hysteria at Brad's skit but as the tension drained out of us in hitching sighs and wiped eyes it was rapidly replaced with a feeling of awkwardness. We were all strangers, to Amsterdam and to each other and nobody knew what to say. Everyone was waiting for someone else to break the silence, a silence that was becoming almost deafening in the small room. I racked my brain for something, anything to say. It was impossible to know where to pitch the conversation. Getting to know you chit chat seemed perverse somehow. We'd all introduced ourselves but asking someone how they managed to end up in this hell-scape seemed indecorous. There were more pertinent questions to be asked but they seemed worse, bringing the horror and the danger back into the room; Where were you when it happened? Did you see anyone get killed? How many of your own party have you lost? Keith's face loomed in the forefront of my mind. I hoped he was safe. I felt sick that we'd left him behind to fend for himself.

It felt wild to me that only yesterday I had been chasing my cold beer with hot crispy Kaasstengels and idly wondering about whether or not I should become a YouTube travel guide after having so much fun with my internal monologue. It had been a pleasant daydream but would have taken a dark turn on the latest part of this trip; "Hey guys, so what do you do if you're watching two strangers do it on-stage and a violent pandemic breaks out. Coming up next! Don't forget to like and subscribe!"

"So," Ross said, slapping his knees, the sound as loud and shocking as a gunshot in the silent room. It made me flinch, ducking my head for cover. "You gonna share?" he asked Jake, seemingly unaware of the effect he'd had on everyone else, cocking his head at the half rolled joint underneath Jake's trembling fingers.

In that moment I was half furious, that all Ross could think about was getting off his tits, and half relieved that someone, even if it had been him, had broken the oppressive silence. Jake looked at him petulantly and continued creating a quite impressive looking cone. It was like a piece of structural engineering, a skyscraper made of spit and Rizla. He folded and twisted, engrossed in his task. Most of us (apart from the catatonic Meg) began to watch him, equally absorbed in his project. Jake's small, pink tongue flicked out of his mouth like a snake to wet each piece of paper before securing it in place. Finally, smoothing his fingers along its length, Jake seemed to deem it complete. He held it up, twisting it under the fluorescent lights so we could all gaze at it in awe. I half expected an marvelling "oooooh" like at a firework display. It was oddly hypnotic. Flicking his lighter, Jake put the joint in his mouth and took a couple of small tokes at it, letting the flame take hold and releasing fragrant smoke to coil into the air.

The smell was a welcome reprieve in the confines of the coffee-shop. As a group, we stunk. The overriding smell was sweat, from both fear and exertion. The second was the fug of damp laundry still emanating from Tim, albeit like damp laundry a sweaty tramp had rolled around on for a bit first, while eating a hunk of ripe cheese. I thought the lingering smell of cheese was in my imagination until I saw Tommy emptying his pockets. Unbeknownst to the rest of us, while we'd been gawping at the carnage out on the street, Tommy had been grabbing a good selection of snacks from the cheese shop. Each chunk of cheese bore its own identification sticker. Out came Gouda, Leyden, Maasdam, a little pot of chutney, a box of crackers. I started laughing, the little titbits and treats kept coming, like a magician's handkerchief out of the never-ending Tardis-like vacuum of his pockets.

He shrugged "I really did have the munchies eh?" his smile turned down at the edges and trembled perilously on his lips.

A couple of hours ago, we'd been having fun. This should have been something we were laughing about all together. But now we were a band of survivors in a little black box missing one of our members and it didn't feel as though anything would be funny ever again. I tried to imagine Keith in my mind's eye, quaffing champagne with a gaggle of beautiful women, safe and secure and waiting for rescue. Maybe if I willed it hard enough then the universe would do me a solid and it would come true. I tried really hard to imagine it but every time my eyes closed I saw the thing that had once been a man, snapping chunks out of the shopkeeper's arm. I tried to shake the image away but it was there like a sunspot, transposed on the back of my eyelids. I desperately needed to not think, just for a little while. Where had that spliff got to?

Jake had dutifully passed the joint left to Ross, who was sucking on it like an infant with a bottle. He watched me walk over, warily tracking every step like a dog guarding a bone. I didn't have the capacity to be polite, to wait my turn and hope it made it to me. Knowing Ross he'd smoke the lot out of spite, rather than share. I didn't feel like Captain Boy Scout, a kind kindergarten teacher, a goody-two-shoes or any of the other things Ross had derided me about or with. I felt jangly and disconnected, like a man on a mission to find some oblivion before doing something really stupid, like punching a team mate in the face. Plucking the monster bifter from his fingers I ignored his indignant protestations. He was far too stoned to stand and fight for the thing back but maybe he also realised squaring off to me at this point would have been a fool's errand. I had not only height, but solid weight on him. It wasn't something I usually threw around. But for Ross I'd make an exception.

Drawing deeply on it, I let the searing smoke fill up my lungs, before coughing it out in a stream towards the ceiling. I took a smaller toke the second time, holding my breath like I'd seen in the movies. I didn't cough as much on the second exhale. Ignoring Ross's outstretched hand, demanding the joint back, I walked it over to Jennifer. The effects were almost instant, my legs felt like wet spaghetti and my head swam pleasantly. I rubbed my chest at the burnt feeling at its centre. Having never even smoked cigarettes before I was unused to the sensation. Jennifer sat on one of the banquettes, two tea towels, stolen from behind the counter, looped around her bloodied hands. She looked at the joint in my fingers and seemed to be considering trying to take it with her towelled mittens. I had horrible visions of them going up in flames, but before I could say anything she dropped one and closed two fingers around the joint, on a hand that looked like raw meat. She nodded back towards Ross who, realising he wasn't going to get the skyscraper back, was building another joint out of Jake's supplies. He was seemingly oblivious to the dark look Jake was giving him as he rifled through his paraphernalia.

"Sorry Joe but your mate is an absolute bellend. If this was a horror movie he'd be the first one getting bit and not telling anyone until it was too late so the rest of them didn't lop his head off," she whispered out of the side of her mouth.

I couldn't have agreed more. I had no doubt Ross was the kind of person who would save his own skin, even at the expense of others. I didn't trust him one little bit. She gave the joint back to me and I sat down next to her, pulling more smoke deep into my lungs and surveying the room. I could see a couple more Rizla megastructures circulating in the group. Leaning back against the banquette I tried to concentrate on the smoke dancing and twirling in the air above me and the numbing feeling crawling through my veins.

The weed was certainly helping to thaw the atmosphere. People were starting to relax and conversation was tentatively beginning to open up, like fiddlehead ferns unfurling. Michael, Brad, Ian, Charlie and Jake were also on a stag do but they'd lost the rest of their group including the stag. I didn't want to ask what they specifically meant by lost but from the look on Ian's face it seemed evident that they hadn't simply been split up. Kate told us, while still rubbing Meg's back in rhythmic circles, that they had flown over from States earlier in the week, hoping to get settled and have a bit of a holiday before term was due to begin at their exchange university. They hadn't been able to get in touch with any of their fellow students on campus or their family back home to see if the same thing was happening in the US as well. The idea stopped me cold, drying up all the saliva in my already perilously dry mouth. I had, up to now, assumed it was just an isolated incident and we'd get out of the city and all would be well. I hadn't even thought about it spreading or happening in other places. I couldn't fathom that this could be the new normal and I'd have to learn to survive without any modern amenities. I'd been moaning about sharing a bathroom in a hostel, how was I going to cope having to go back to shitting in the woods and brushing my teeth with my finger like a cave man? Were we going to have to set up civilisation from scratch again?

I wanted to let my thoughts idly wander, give myself a break, but the idea that the phenomenon we were currently experiencing might well be all over the world had gotten under my skin and wriggled in, laying eggs of doubt like a bot fly. The weed wasn't doing much to dampen the thought, but was in fact making it bigger, scarier. I had to stand, get moving, anything not to be alone with the all encompassing thought that the world as I had known it was over. Wandering around the room, I tried to get involved in conversations but the thought kept popping up like Whack-a-mole. I had to know what was going on but my phone was now more use as a weapon than as a source of information. Looking around the room for inspiration, I found it high up on the wall in the form of a small mounted TV. I let out a little exclamation, overjoyed at finding hopefully another source of knowledge in the unexpected desert of information we had currently found ourselves in.

Crossing my fingers behind my back, I hoped for a news programme, a bulletin, anything that might shed some light on what was going on. I needed to know the extent of the crisis and the time scale for resolution. Surely there would be a group of officials or scientists in a bunker somewhere with a machine spitting out reams of paper telling them exactly how to fix the problem and turn everyone back. They'd pass on the information to a world leader who would be on the TV reassuring us all in dulcet tones, giving us the idiot's guide to the plan. Or it would already be over and we'd been hiding for no reason. We could emerge into the frosty night, amongst beery revellers and locals going for a late dinner, feeling sheepish that we'd thought it the end of the world. There would be consoling policeman and clean up crews to dispose of evidence that anything had even happened. But then I remembered the wave of people running, the creatures looping in and out of them, people crashing onto the cobbles. I remembered the carpet of the dead as we made our way to this place. I doubted it had been resolved but I couldn't help but hope. I needed hope.

Ferreting around behind the coffee-shop counter I found the remote control, nestled in beside the cash register. Although remotes are an almost universal bit of kit, no two ever seem to look or function the same. I closed one eye to focus and jabbed at all of the buttons, changing the output to HDMI, over to Satellite and back to AV1 with nothing but a stoic blue screen. I kept jabbing. Suddenly the TV blared into life, much too loud for the tight confines of the room and the delicate state of the group. I hammered my thumb onto the volume control, bringing the noise down to just barely loud enough to hear. I didn't want to advertise our presence here any more than we already had and I didn't want to give any of us a heart attack. My own heart leapt painfully into my dry throat at the sight of the words **"Nooduitzending – Emergency Broadcast"** scrolling across the bottom of the screen. Maybe my prayers had been answered.

It wasn't the prime minister or a sober looking scientist but a terrified looking newscaster in a suit so rumpled she must have slept in it. Her hair was escaping her slick bun and her eyes were wild. That couldn't be a good thing. She haltingly read from a single piece of paper in Dutch. It was interminable to listen to her lilting cadence and to not know what she was saying. After a pause to check the back of the paper for more information, she re-read it, this time in English. I didn't realise I was holding my breath until my vision began swimming at the edges. I let it out in a dry huff. She told us that the city was in a state of emergency, that it was imperative we stay inside and wait for help. And that was it. Details of how and when the help were going to appear were glaringly absent. I flicked the channels over. The face of the person reading the announcement was different but the words were exactly the same. The meaning in between the statements was the same. We were marooned. In a city full of water we had been cast adrift, shipwrecked and left waiting for rescue. The only advice was to keep staring at the horizon and pray a rescue vessel came over it soon. I'd read, a thousand years ago in an airport hotel, that there were over a million people in Amsterdam, not including fluctuations in tourists. It was going to take a long time to sweep the city and rescue that many people. Unless there are not that many people alive. That horrifying thought dropped on my chest like a boulder, squashing all of the remaining air from my seared lungs.

I was jittery with panic. The room was too small to pace. It seemed too full. Full of fearful looking people and the missing words from the report, bumping up against each other like helium balloons. Sitting at one of the tables, facing away from the television set, I started trying to roll a joint from the provisions left there. It was a mess. It looked like an animal begging to be put out of its misery. The end tapered down to a snout or beak and the edges curled upwards, threatening to spill its contents onto the sticky table. I hadn't used enough spit to keep its sides together since there didn't seem to be enough left in my mouth. I didn't care. I lit the monstrosity and held the smoke in my lungs until my heartbeat beat a tattoo in my temples. I felt like I was trying to urge the THC through my veins, to block out the thoughts and drown those unspoken words. I needed to be oblivious to the situation. Just for a little bit.

**

I'm surprised at the amount of detail Jennifer is going into. She's a great storyteller but I don't know how she can stand it. The memories she evokes with her words are a knife; painful and sharp inside me. I feel each delicate slice like she is trying to peel back my skin. It's one of the reasons I've always been vague with Amelia about exactly what happened out there. I do everything I can to stop the sudden razor-sharp incision of memories digging into my flesh. Sometimes it's an association or a sound but a smell can be just as powerful.

The odour of weed is endemic in England. You'll be minding your own business and someone will walk past you on the street, or at the bus stop, trailing the scent behind them, like the tail of a comet. Or you'll walk past a house and the whiff of it will leak out from under the door or waft out of a window. It is a quintessential part of British life, like bemoaning the cost of a Freddo or the pathological urge to queue and tut loudly at those who do not. The smell of it doesn't remind me of saying something stupid or waking up in a bush, like tequila does. The smell of it makes me feel a rush of panic, like my whole body has pins and needles.

The smell of weed reminds me of the morning I killed someone.

If only Joe had never found that remote. I know what happened next wasn't really his fault but I would have loved to have lived my rose-coloured fantasy for just a couple of hours more. In it we would have turned the television on and seen how the emergency was over and there was a toll free number on the rolling banner that you could ring and register your interest for a rescue. You are number six in the queue, a tiny automated voice would pronounce. An hour later, enough time to smoke up a little more, a friendly man in a high-vis jacket would knock briskly on the door, holding a clipboard and some of those shiny blankets you get after a marathon. He and his colleagues would bundle us into waiting minivans and take us to the nearest plush hotel for warm baths and hot meals, on the house. Maybe the hotel would give us spa vouchers and we'd have a lovely time before our flights back to the real world. I didn't want reality. Not just yet. But there I was craning my neck to see a woman scared out of her wits, reading a pre-prepared report that didn't seem to say an awful lot. It was merely an extension of the emergency alert message my, now useless, phone had sent me hours before. Her terrified eyes haunted me. They were the opposite of reassuring. Looking around the room it was evident the report had sucked all of the hope out of the air like oxygen in a house fire.

Pandora's box was well and truly opened so we left the TV on. No-one wanted a return to silence, that would mean we would have to fill it, have to talk about what we had just seen. Around midnight the newsreader changed. A man in a far less crumpled suit took the woman's place and read out the same report. Around 2 a.m the newsreader changed again. This lady didn't look scared, she looked angry. She ditched the pre-written report and instead went live to a reporter in the field. From the commotion in the studio it seemed unlikely it was planned. The field reporter had a flak jacket with PRESS on the front, and a helmet with a chin strap. It was the kind of outfit I'd seen on stories that had the sound of mortar fire in the background.

The camera panned to one of the squares, full of army personnel and roadblocks. The reporter advised that roadblocks had been placed around the city. As though I had willed it, a barrage of gun fire burst out of the small TV speakers, making us all jump. Behind the reporter, the soldiers began to fire into an approaching column of the creatures. There was shouting from the crew. The screen went black. Picking up the remote from Joe's table and I clicked off the TV. The only sound in the room was Kate softly crying.

The night devolved from there. We needed to fill the vacuum that absence of hope had sucked away. Joe had fallen on Jake's bag of weed but we were all clamouring to get involved. The bag was small and the joints rolled were strong and was down to crumbs in minutes. Without saying a word Ross left his seat, weaving and meandering to a door marked 'Privaat' behind the counter. Before the door had fully swung shut behind him, I heard him shout out. Shit. I had no idea if anyone had checked back there yet. For all we knew there could have been one of those things hiding there, biding its time and now currently eating Ross alive. Standing shakily, I grabbed onto the metal serviette dispenser on the table with difficulty, trying to ignore the pain of the cold metal pressed into my flesh. I walked forward, my hand extending slowly for the handle.

Ross slammed back through the door, almost knocking me over in his excitement to show us his haul. His arms were laden with bags and bags of marijuana, both pre-rolled and loose. The dispenser slipped slickly out of my sweaty palm, falling to the carpet. I was so angry. That thoughtless, selfish arse. I wished I had pitched it at him. The thought of the hollow bonk as it bounced off his head elicited a thin, precarious smile on my face. That would have to do. That smile got considerably larger when I saw the loot that he carried in, and dumped, on one of the central tables. It looked like we were going to have ourselves a bit of a party. Or a wake.

Ross, Jake and Charlie set up a very close approximation to a production line. They pulled two tables together, hastily wiped them down, and sat next to each other on one of the banquettes. One man ground the bags of green with a small plastic grinder, one sprinkled and the other licked and rolled the joint into existence. The neat little cones began to gather at one end of the table, stacked against each other. They were surprisingly fast. A laugh burbled out of me when Charlie slapped Tim's hand away from the rapidly increasing pile, like a mother smacking a toddler's hand reaching for the cookies. But there was a slight twinge of guilt as the pile increased. We were stealing after all. But it wasn't the first petty larceny I'd committed today and it paled in comparison with all of the murder we'd witnessed. Still, I thought morbidly, if we died here no-one would get in trouble for some light theft. In for a penny, in for a pound.

Once the production line were satisfied, the boys sat back and looked at their spread. It truly was a thing of beauty. They didn't get to admire their handy-work for long, as the rest of the group fell on the pile like a starving man on a buffet. Soon the small room resembled the scene of a chip pan fire; a dense fog that hung low and cloying in the air. As we sat back and relaxed with our joints, hesitant conversation started up. No-one mentioned the television reports. Tim and John were engaged in a very uninspiring conversation about the Champions League, so I wandered off, trailing my own purple tinged fug to a table where Brad seemed to be butchering a magic trick. As he lost and picked up the thread of his spiel multiple times I watched Kate's mouth fall open, transfixed at the magic unfolding, not noticing the various bungles. Even the near catatonic Meg was following his hands, the one eye not pressed against the cushions, open and tracking him. As bright as a cat's eye in the dim light.

My mouth tasted like the bottom of a handbag so I went to look for something cold to drink in the industrial, hip height fridges which buzzed pleasantly behind the counter. I kicked something solid and heard Joe yowl from his cross legged position on the floor. He'd been staring into the kaleidoscope of colours of the juice bottles, gently sweating from the sliding door being open too long.

"What are you looking for?" I asked him, my mouth sticking together with every word.

"I really wanted a beer," said his almost disembodied voice from the floor.

In my rational, cognizant mind, somewhere way at the back, I knew it was illegal for coffee-shops to serve alcohol. But my stoned mind currently sitting front and centre didn't know how to articulate that thought.

"No beer. Bad. Illegal. Juice. Juice!" I exclaimed at the top of Joe's head. We laughed stupidly and breathlessly for what felt like an age. Hanging on weakly to the counter, an ugly caw brayed from between my lips. We were well and truly stuck in a case of the giggles and it felt great, like a great pressure valve had released.

It took a while, but after regaining a semblance of control over my body again I tottered back over to the seats with a bottle of juice and tried to sink back in the worn velvet of the banquette. The weighted blanket feeling of being stoned was a comfort. It muffled my thoughts, like trying to think through a thick layer of snow. I sipped at the juice. It tasted amazing, tingling on my tongue.

I might have been able to relax, maybe even getting some sleep if I hadn't been jostled awake every time my head nodded by exclamations from the table next to mine. Rolling my head to the side I tried to concentrate on what was going on. The discussion between Charlie, Jake and Ross had ramped up in its intensity. They curved in on another, jabbing their fingers in each other's glassy eyed faces, with an almost violent severity. It did not pass the vibe check. Their conversation was not giggly and muffled, it was bubbling and bordering on spilling over. The Fear, peaked over my shoulder, whispering in my ear that the fervent conversation was definitely, unequivocally about me.

Sliding over to their table, the short distance feeling like a yawning chasm that had to be waded through like jelly, I was thoroughly convinced that I was about to hear their plan on how to get rid of me. It seemed obvious. I'd crashed in through the window of their safe hiding place and made them run for their lives on the street. Of course they would want to get shot of me. My heart rocketed into my throat as I caught snatches of their whisper-shouted conversation.

"YOU'RE SO RIGHT!"

"TOTALLY!"

"YES!"

"DEFINITELY FAKE NEWS!"

The last exclamation halted my accelerating

breath with a wet hitch. My brain, so heavily doused in THC, was struggling to make sense of how I, Jennifer Sawson, could be fake news. I inched in closer. They didn't even notice me, they were too focused on each other's faces.

"You're so right. It's absolutely fake news. There is no way that's real," said Charlie, spittle flecking his chin as he nodded at Ross.

"Yeah man. Gotta be crisis actors," Jake nodded sagely. My addled brain couldn't catch up. I had no idea what or who they were talking about.

"FAKE NEWS!" Ross reiterated delightedly and incredibly loudly. No longer surreptitious, his yell making everyone jump.

"It's a liberal conspiracy theory to keep the sheep scared and compliant," nodded Charlie "Come on I'll show you," he said, standing up and gesturing his head to the stairs that led down to the barricaded front door.

My mouth popped open in disbelief. Surely he was going to get to the top step and shout something like "Psych! Nah fooled ya! That would be stupid. I don't want to get eaten. Obvs" There was no way he was serious, was there? Surely it was an elaborate prank and the other two wouldn't be so gullible to fall for it. Jake and Ross left the table and joined Charlie, who was removing the furniture in front of the stairs, down to the barricaded door.

I waited for Charlie to laugh and turn round, back into the safe, warm womb of the room, willing it to happen with all of my strength at the back of his head. But it didn't happen. He took the first step, then the second, on and on his body disappeared from view. Jake and Ross followed him. Looking around the room, the shock of their departure was plastered on the faces of everybody else. This was real. It was happening. Dragging my tired, heavy body to the top of the stairs, I watched as the little group kept going. I had to stop them. Hammering down the steps behind them against the exhaustion of the days exercise in my wobbly thighs as well as the weed in my system trying to slow me down. The world tipped and lurched in my vision. I held onto the bannister with a death grip, scared all my muscles were going to cramp at once and send me plummeting down the stairs to break my neck at the bottom.

"You can't be serious!" I shouted behind them. A vision of John McEnroe floating up behind my eyes. The weed was still playing word association games with my thoughts. It made me want to bark with laughter but it was far from funny. "Don't be stupid, you'll be killed!" I tried again.

Charlie looked back up at me and snorted in derision. His face was pulled up into a nasty grin, devoid of humour. The Fear poked me in the ribs and told me that I was in danger. It whispered in my ear that it was a ploy to get rid of me after all. They were going to lure me down to the bottom of the stairs and push me outside, shutting the door behind me. All I'd hear would be the men laughing at my desperate cries to be let back in and the creatures getting closer and closer behind me, stalking me for the kill. It was as clear to me as a movie projected on the foyer wall. I gripped onto the bannister even tighter as Charlie took a step towards me. His hot, rancid breath blew across my face, making my nose wrinkle in disgust, as he leaned in close.

"Typical brain-washed, scaredy little, precious snowflake," he said, rolling his eyes "You believe everything the media tells you? It's all fake. You'll see. We're going to go out there and all of the crisis actors will part like the red sea. They won't be able to hurt actual civilians. Those "victims" were wearing blood packs and prosthetics and shit. It's all fake news" he said condescendingly, making quotation marks in the air with his fingers.

The fine mist of his spittle landed on my cheek. I wanted to wipe it away didn't want to scare him with any sudden movements, like a wild animal, dangerous and unpredictable. His eyes search my face before he steps away from me and back into the waiting circle of Ross and Jake.

"What a libtard," Ross said rolling his eyes and laughing at me. He clapped Charlie on the back.

The fight went out of me and my body plonked down onto the step, half way up. I had no idea how to reply. Trying to disprove their tin-foil hat thinking was beyond my current ken.

"God speed dum-dums," I said to their backs, still quivering with mirth at my supposed naivety. They didn't hear me. I wasn't sure if I really cared.

Charlie and Ross pulled back the makeshift barricade, leaving it next to the door. I kept my eye on it. The boys might be convinced about going outside, but we needed people ready to get the barricade back in place as soon as they realised their mistake and came back in.

"The fuck is going on?" Brad yelled down from the top of the stairs.

"This group of absolute geniuses is going to go outside to show us that the liberal lefty media is lying about the fricking creatures eating people," I called back up to him.

A lot of shouting ensued. From both sides. There was name calling, emotional appeals, tears and even a little scuffle as Tim and Stuart tried to physically restrain Ross from going outside. But the boys would not be swayed. They had convinced themselves and each other that they were the only ones who really knew the truth and through their actions we'd all be exposed for the brainless sheeple that we were. I could see Ross trying to convince Stuart that he and his new born again believer friends were the only ones in the right. His hand was gripped around Stuart's arm and his words insistent in his ear. I could see Stuart swaying, both on his feet and in his resolve. On the other side of him Joe held onto his shoulder. They were in a human tug of war with their friend. I was relieved when Ross shrugged and relinquish his grip, conceding defeat. We didn't need any more people deciding it was a good idea to go outside. Stuart sunk to the floor, ugly-crying as the barricade was removed. Joe's eyes looked distinctly dry as he watched Ross move towards the door.

**

Tears are welling in my eyes. I look up into the bright lights of the auditorium and try to blink them away before they spill down my cheeks, a trick my mother taught me to preserve my makeup. These days I wear waterproof mascara, because tears are always closer to the surface than they were before, but it's an ingrained habit that comes naturally without really thinking. The lights burn bright spots onto my retinas, and I wish they were hot enough to burn away the guilt that is currently seeping through every cell in my body, leaking out of my pores to mingle with my flop sweat. It makes me want to scratch at my skin like a mangy dog, to make the outside of myself feel like the inside. I want to hurt like I deserve. Looking down at my scarred hands I wonder if I have in fact hurt enough for a life time.

I think about that little glimmer of hope I'd had before the television turned on. I used to be a person that was, if not entirely glass half full, certainly more optimistic than I am now. In that moment what had already happened was bad but there was still some hope that things could get better. Once we saw the report, and once the group of three decided they were the second bloody coming of ultimate truth, things just got worse and worse. Should I have done more to stop them? Could I have done more to stop them?

I have to think a little bit more carefully about the way I tell this story. Do I tell these strangers that I was so scared they were going to lure me out of the door that I didn't try harder to stop them from leaving? Do I admit that I am a coward whose feelings were hurt, so didn't do everything in their power to stop a really bad situation from getting worse? Or do I reveal that for all my bravado I was really pretty impotent in the whole scenario? What is more important? To preserve truth? To find absolution? Or to retain my self worth and sanity? There are choices to make.

It took me longer than I'd like to admit to work out what was going on. I didn't see Ross and the others making their way to the stairs, I was too thoroughly ensconced in my own world. It wasn't until the shouting started that I realised something was happening. The weed had made my thinking slow and cumbersome but when I saw what they were about to do it was as though my brain had taken a dunk in a vat of espresso. I sobered up. Fast. So fast it was like vertigo. Fucking Ross. It was typical that he'd be one of those involved. He was a whirling dervish of a man, whipping up the dust of chaotic energy wherever he went and expecting everyone else to pick up the pieces. He was like a toddler with no sense of danger and while that childlike willingness to jump head-first into any situation was something I could once have admired, after having to babysit him from the moment we got to the airport until now, I could see why parenthood is not for everyone.

As Ross waited for the barrier to be drawn back, he had the slack expression and wild eyes of a man fully converted to a cause. The Kool-Aid had well and truly been drunk. He seemed less the wily weasel that I'd always considered him to be, and now more of a slavering lapdog to his new friends. Even so, I tried to talk him out of it, using everything I could think of. Logic was to no avail and appealing to his ego by telling him he was too smart for this didn't work either. All it garnered me was smirks, silly faces and his seemingly steely resoluteness to keep going with the intended plan. There was nothing I could say to make him see sense and my capacity to care was starting to drain away like water from a cracked cup. Why not just let him do whatever he wanted, like usual. He was (technically) a grown up.

Stuart was beside himself, showing the kind of emotion I'd never seen from him before. I certainly didn't think I'd ever seen him cry before. But here he was, unashamedly blubbering and sniffling in the foyer after failing to convince his best man not to go outside. His best man. Huh. Oh. Ouch. I could feel that particular switch of recognition flicking and it was not a pleasant sensation. Once upon a time, Stuart and I had been nearly inseparable, hanging out after school and at weekends but since he had met Ross they had gotten closer and closer and, after my butting heads with Ross, all but shut me out. It had been insidious and gradual and I hadn't noticed the signs. All of our communication had become one sided. He only ever contacted me if he wanted something, we never hung out without Ross and he never stood up for me when Ross mocked or baited me. Our friendship now listed badly to one side, like a grounded boat. I doubted he would show the same kind of emotion if it had been me that had decided to go outside instead. He probably would have wished me bon bloody voyage and waved me on my way.

Normally I would have engaged in my standard peacekeeping routine, dancing and contorting and stretching myself thin like a rubber band to keep everyone happy with a constant stream of bubbling chatter. But now the assuaging words were sour and limp in my mouth and my lips were reticent to expel them. I was too tired and too heartsick to try. I couldn't. And finally, I wouldn't. A deep embarrassment settled over me at my cringing attempts at group conciliator over the years. I was especially embarrassed at my actions over the bloody stag do. How stupid to be planning Stuart's stag do and dreaming about being his best me before he had even asked me. A case of being over-eager and under-aware the whole time.

Watching Stuart's tears in silence, I so angry that I'd begun to tremble and couldn't trust myself to talk. Stuart and Ross had barely blinked when we'd left Keith behind. There had certainly not been this kind of carry on. Oh Keith. I was so ashamed that I'd not stood up to them both and demanded we do something about Keith. He could be dead now because of my pathetic people pleasing. I raged and seethed at the thought.

Jennifer watched me from her place on the stairs, I could feel the heat of her stare on my face. She was probably wondering why I'd stopped trying to convince the group to stay like the rest of my friends were continuing to do. There were no longer any words or frankly the inclination to keep going. I wasn't their parent and I'd just realised that I was barely even considered a friend, a good one at least. One who wasn't a boring nag. So I sat down on the stairs across from her and watched Ross, Charlie and Jake psych each other up for their expedition. They were approaching it like athletes, stretching their hamstrings and rolling their shoulders, warming up. Ross hopped up and down and whooped like he was about to attempt the one hundred metre sprint, which probably wasn't far from the truth. He kept trying to catch my eye but I purposefully didn't look at him. My rage was at a slow rolling boil and if he started grinning and gurning at me I was quite likely to drive my fist into his face.

Stuart was continuing to hiccup and grizzle miserably in the corner. I couldn't look at him either. I felt sick and helpless and wanted to go back upstairs again, away from their spectacle, but my arse felt as though it was welded to the step. The well of energy needed to push myself back up again felt pretty dry. So I stayed. And waited. And watched.

When the barricade was fully removed and the door finally opened it was amazing to see the foyer fill with weak winter sun. It had become morning without any of us realising it. It left me dazzled and discombobulated. Combined with the weed I felt adrift, detached from reality. Surely I was just imagining the three men bounding out of the door, like children who have been kept at home for too long, full of energy, calling out to and shoving one another? They wouldn't really be so stupid? Would they?

"Close it," Jennifer said monotonously next to me, breaking the spell.

"What?" Brad hissed.

"Just push it closed. I'm not saying lock it but just close it until they're ready to come back. Having it wide open like that is awful," she shivered.

When Brad didn't move Jennifer stood and stepped forward to push the door closed with the flat of her forearm herself. I knew exactly what she meant. Having the door wide open, with no idea as to what was on the other side, gave me palpitations. We almost didn't get it closed last time and having it swinging wild in the wind felt like an open invitation to let flesh eaters through the door for an all-you-can-eat buffet.

I joined her at the door and together we pushed our faces up against the small port hole window. The conspiracy theory brigade frolicked in the deserted street. They pushed each other further and further out, daring each other like little boys, laughing and shrieking the whole time. They were so loud I could hear them through the door, above the thundering of my own heartbeat in my ears.

The doublethink was incredible. It was gobsmacking. How could any of them, but especially Ross, not believe what was happening. I didn't know what the others had seen but I had stood beside Ross as we watched a man broken apart and consumed with the voracity that a drunk attacks a bargain bucket at Chicken Cottage at 3 a.m. What kind of cognitive dissonance did it take to witness that with your own two eyes and still label it fake? Did he really think that man was in a green room somewhere taking off his SFX makeup with baby wipes and having a nice cup of tea? It might have been funny if it hadn't been so bloody infuriating and so irresponsibly dangerous. Not just dangerous for him and his new pals, but also for the

rest of us watching, standing behind one flimsy
door twitching to put the barricade back in place.

I was so angry. So tired and hungry and stoned-
over and sad that I couldn't stop myself. Opening
the door, the frigid wind hitting me in the face, I
took a deep breath.

"COME BACK INSIDE THIS INSTANT!" I
yelled, leaning forward and pushing the air through
my lungs, my vocal cords and my mouth as hard as
possible.

The sound was catastrophically loud in the
empty street. It ricocheted against buildings and
stampeded down pavements. It swooped across
canal surfaces and roused birds into the air. It roared
in the small confines of the vestibule. If the burn of
the exhalation hadn't been scorching my throat as I
sucked in the cold outside air, I wouldn't have
believed that noise had come out of me. Looking
around, no one else seemed to be able to believe it
either. Every person in the foyer gawped at me and
in the street, the three men stared back at me too,
their eyes wide and shocked.

"Are you fucking seriou..." Jake managed before
the first of the creatures rounded the corner.

It threw its body mindlessly at him, with no

sense of its own preservation. They both crashed to the pavement, cutting Jake's words off with a yip of terror. The crash of bone and skull connecting with the pavement was both heavy and wet. The thing gripped and tore at Jake's defensive arms with its broken and mangled fingers, desperate to get at the soft meat of Jake's face. It didn't take long to connect. The creature was much stronger than him and it was caught in the paroxysms of blood lust. Jake's screams were curdled and hysterical.

Charlie tried to kick the thing off him, but he might as well have been kicking a brick wall for all the difference it made. None of his blows even turned the head of the bloodied hellion ripping into his friend. He may as well have not even been there. Charlie kept trying. He was so intent on saving Jake that he didn't notice the thundering of footsteps towards them. Ross did. Even at this distance I could see the horror in his face. He understood, terribly and completely, that the creatures were not the product of a conspiracy theory. They were very, very real and they were coming. He was close enough to be splattered with the fine raindrops of Jake's blood, to smell the viscera. There could be no faking that.

Ross didn't stop to help Jake, who was now limp and split open like over-ripe fruit on the cold cobbles. He didn't stop to help Charlie either, who was now fighting off his own assailant. It wasn't clear whether he knew it was too late for them, or whether he was only thinking of his own skin. I'll never know. There were so many of them, so quickly.

The things, that had once been tourists or residents had fallen on his new friends like a flock of seagulls on a spilled bag of chips. They snapped and snarled at one another in their desperation to get their fill of the spoils. Jake had stopped screaming a while ago and Charlie didn't scream for long, the creatures making short work of them both. But Ross screamed. He screamed all the way back towards the closed door of the coffee-shop. His cries did not go unnoticed. The creatures on the edge of the scrum, trying to get to the once living banquet, saw their opportunity for food and gave chase. There were only a few feet between Ross and their snapping jaws. They took off after him, moving unselfconsciously and at full tilt, not caring or slowing down if they fell. They kept moving towards their prey at all times, on hands and elbows and knees and thighs until they could get up again and continue their pursuit.

Ross wailed and yelled, pumping his legs as hard as he could to get back to the coffee-shop. We watched. The door stayed shut between us. He called for us to open up, to let him back in. The door stayed shut between us. The reverberations of sound pulsed through the wood as Jennifer and I leant against it, watching him through the window. Neither of us moved. The door stayed shut between us.

**

Oh shit. Oh shit. As Jennifer gets to this part in our shared story the shame crawls up my legs like an army of ants, encircling my torso, skittering over my face and into my scalp. My flesh creeps, tightening over my entire body and heating up until it's like I'm being boiled from the inside out. At first, listening to Jennifer reveal all was mesmerising and horrifying at the same time. I knew she would get to this part in the story but now that we're at the destination, the inevitability of it is no comfort. Soon she'll tell this entire audience, including Amelia, what we did, what decisions we made and their consequences. When it happens, when the bomb is dropped, I am expecting Amelia's hand to slip out of my clammy grasp, and her face to turn to me in a mask of contempt. I am waiting for the one person in the world who knows and understands me best to turn their back on me because I am not the man she thought she knew. I expect her to tell me that I'm the devil and deserve to die alone. I don't

211

think I would disagree.

Listening and waiting, knowing what is coming, is torture. But I can not stand up and move away. I want to. Desperately. I want to stand up and start running. Run away from the words that I know are coming, run down the stairs, just starting to go threadbare in the middle from the travel of too many feet, through the double doors at the bottom, out onto the drizzling pavement and into the crowded streets. I want to lose myself and keep running away from the man I brought back from Amsterdam. I don't move. I wait. Even now, I'm so angry at Ross for putting me in this situation. I'm angry at Jennifer for breaking our pact and invoking his spirit in this room. But mostly I'm angry at myself for being a coward, both then and now. I seethe. I wait.

CHAPTER SEVENTEEN: JENNIFER

Jonah's shout was so loud it made my ears ring, like a bad case of tinnitus. I was shocked. He didn't seem like the kind of person to lose his temper in such a manner. True, I hadn't known him for long but I thought I was a pretty good judge of character and had found him to be calm and reasonable so far. His friend had called him Captain Boyscout. That's not the kind of nickname that is given to a hot-head who flips out at the drop of a hat. I was sure I wasn't wrong about him. I'd got the number of both Stuart and Ross ever since I had crashed, quite literally through the glass of, their party. I'd met plenty of guys like Stuart in my time. They all wore the same uniform; too tight trousers, or too tight shirts, shoes with no socks and an almost heady amount of cologne. Enough that your eyes water and you can taste it in the back of your throat. They have expensive haircuts and branded trainers. They call you "love" and "sweetheart" and look mock hurt when you pull them up on it. They try to tell you it's their dialect or a term of affection, or some other guff, desperate to put you on the back foot, looking like a typical crazy girl. They slide into your booth at the pub when it is obvious that it's a girl's night out. They try to get in your pants even though they know full well there is a girlfriend waiting for them at home, willing to smile indulgently and pop a glass of water and a packet of paracetamol next to the bed, because they know they'll be rough in the morning. And they call you a frigid bitch if you refuse them. They are the kind of men who try to tell you they are the nice guys because they want you to let your guard down around them. I've met Stuart before in many iterations, in many jobs and bars and queues in late night taxi ranks. More often than not they are accompanied by a Ross or two.

The Stuarts aren't great but they pale in comparison with the Ross's of the world. Those are the kind of guys who smack your arse as you're walking past and then tell you you're being too sensitive. That it's a compliment. They're the guys who tell you at the end of a long working day when you're standing at the bus stop that you'd be really pretty if you just smiled and wait expectantly in front of you until you do just that. They are the kind of guys that you find yourself fake laughing with or trying not to piss off because if you hurt their feelings they will more than likely turn nasty. They make jokes at your expense and expect to be praised for them. A Ross will slide up to you on the dance floor and thrust themselves just a bit too close and leer at you like you're a bit of meat. He will try to block your escape when you try to leave the situation, using his body as a tool of intimidation. They always get their own way and if they don't they get angry at a moment's notice and lose their complete shit over something small. This Ross is finally understanding what it means to be looked at like a bit of meat. He is little more than a running buffet to the creatures who hound him at this point.

Those abominations were busily tearing into Charlie and Jake like they were something soft and yielding, rather than skin, bone and muscle. I could see them stuffing bits of the boys into their mouths and fighting over the chunks left behind, snapping at each other like rabid dogs. How could anyone could think their appearances were just really good makeup and great acting, even in their wildest imaginations. One of the creatures munching on Jake's denim covered leg, was missing most of the side of her own face. I could see the way the sinews and tendons of her jaw were powering her ever-chewing teeth, a constant masticating maw. The marble white, winter sky could clearly be seen through the gaps in her cheek. That was not make-up. I don't think you'd even be able to achieve something that detailed with CGI. She grappled with the limb, fighting off her dinner guests for another bite, tearing through the tough denim like tissue paper. They snarled like hyenas over the people I'd been hanging out with just twenty minutes beforehand, now reduced to nothing more than carrion on the street.

The feasting had given Ross a little bit of extra time to get moving, but it was probably only seconds at best. Those scavenging few who were looking for an in to the main meal, or gobbling up scraps from the pavement, were alerted to Ross's presence by his loud caterwauling. If he'd been quieter, sneakier, maybe he could have gotten away with it. He might have been able to inch past the things on tip toes like in a *Scooby Do* cartoon. Instead, he sprinted towards us, back to the safety of the coffee-shop, making no moves to keep quiet. Joe and I were still leaning on the door watching it all unfold, like a terrible interactive horror movie in front of us, the worst kind of choose-your-own-adventure.

"What the fuck are you doing?! Open the door!" Brad screamed.

I looked back outside and saw the tidal wave of death building behind Ross, threatening to crash down on him, the same way it did on Jake and Charlie. They were so close behind him, he was tripping over their grabbing hands. If we managed by some feat to get Ross into the building, what was there to stop that wave of death crashing in the foyer of the coffee-shop and drowning the rest of us too? I looked back at Brad, knowing that he could see the hesitation in my face, in my unmoving arms, which were still pressed against the door and not moving towards the handle.

"No. You can't! He's a fucking human being! You can't leave him out there to die!" Michael shouted behind me. I still didn't move.

"And what about the rest of us?" said a voice I didn't recognise. Meg.

The girl that looked as though she just going to remain curled into a tight little ball till the end of time was standing at the top of the stairs. I'd not yet heard her speak a single word since we'd been there.

"If we let him in he's going to bring all of those.....those...things in with him and we'll all be killed. Is that what you want? Is his life worth more than all of ours?" she could have been speaking the words already nestled in my head, dangerous and coiled like a viper.

I didn't want to die and I was going to do everything in my power to make sure that didn't happen. But would I do that even if that meant sacrificing someone else? My self preservation was a strong, tangible thing. A baser instinct that I was struggling to ignore, no matter how many societal norms it butted up against.

"This is bullshit," Stuart said, pushing through

the clamouring group and grabbing onto my shoulder.

Seizing at his hand as best I could, I dug my nails into his fingers, clawing at him to let go of me, anything to keep the door blocked. I grappled and scratched at him, like a cat backed into a corner. He was a lot stronger than me and threw me easily out of the way. The only person left in front of the door was Joe. He was a physical boundary line, standing between his people on either side of the door. From my vantage point on the floor, I could see his feet were planted firmly, shoulder width apart. His mouth was set in a bitter, taught line. He looked resolute and formidable. Joe was lean. He was not skinny like the boys I dated in the early noughties – emaciated, with almost concave chests and a flop of hair over delicate features. He was lean in a way that said carbs were not his friend, but the gym was. He was thin in a hard, solid way. He held out his hand and pulled me to my feet in front of the door. I tried not to hiss from the pain in my hands, tried to look as strong as him.

Stuart and Joe stood across from each other, but before either could make a move the door began to shake and rattle as Ross began banging on the other side. The door shook. I could feel it in the tense muscles in my back and shoulders as I leaned against it. The wood did nothing to dampen the sounds of his crying and begging. I felt sick. I didn't want him to die. It was true that I didn't like him very much but I would never have wished him dead. Be that as it may, I didn't want to die either. I categorically refused to die in that place. It was not spite to not let him in it was self preservation. It didn't mean that I didn't feel like a monster, with hot tears on my cheeks, standing sentinel at a grave. There were tears streaking the faces of every person standing in the small foyer. The room was heavy with the scent of our brined sorrow but I couldn't move away from the door. I couldn't let death in to this place. Suddenly Ross stopped sobbing and moaning to be let in. He started shrieking.

**

I'm here. At the part of the story I have been dreading ever since my stupid decision to retell it in its entirety. There is a choice to be made. Two paths stretch away in front of me. The first is to tell this audience that I stood stock still, my body braced against the door and stopped a real live human being from being able to return to a place of safety. It is to tell them that I consciously made that decision, that it didn't happen by accident. I can explain my reasoning for it any which way until I am blue in the face. But the bald, ugly truth will remain. No matter how nicely I try to dress it up and disseminate it. I can tell these waiting faces that I felt Ross hit the door, that I felt the creatures as they slammed into him. I can tell them that I heard his shrieks turn to howling, and that I listened, that we all listened in total silence to a man with whom some of us had only known for a few hours, but for others an actual friend with shared history, being eaten alive by what can only be described as the living dead. I can tell them that, and I can endure their reactions, their words, their recriminations and the consequences that being honest entails. I could do that or I could lie.

It seems self preservation will always be my default setting. I'm going to go with the lie. Looking up into the tiny crescent moon faces of the audience I begin to tell them the sanitised version. In it, three members of our group went out to scout the area and see what was going on. Those brave souls were set upon and killed before anyone could do anything to save them. I struggle through the words, they're acrid in my mouth, like burning leaves on my tongue, threatening to choke me. I push through the shame sitting heavily in my chest and try desperately not to cry. If I start crying now I might never stop.

"Keep it vague. No details," calls out a shaking voice somewhere in the auditorium.

My head snaps round, trying to find its owner. A part of me is genuinely scared this is some wild PTSD manifestation of my own conscience. Or had I said it myself out loud? Goose-flesh jumps out on my back, both cold and hot like a nasty case of flu. The phrase I have been desperately trying to remember hangs in the dusty air, in a voice that is not my own. A figure near the back of the room stands. I hadn't noticed him before. He looks different, greyer, thinner and he's wearing an oversized plain hoodie.

"Joe," I croak.

It's the phrase we'd agreed on at the airport. We'd repeated it over and over to each other before we were separated, to make sure we didn't forget in the midst of the army's questioning. We agreed to keep our recollections of the events we witnessed vague, to not give them any more details than we had to. I'd blocked it out, or forgotten, or repressed it to the deep parts of my memory where Ross's screams play on a loop.

Joe slowly walks down the stairs, makes his way to the bottom of the stage and starts to pull himself up over the hot footlights. The sound engineer starts to make his panicked way over to stop Joe's approach and I flap at him, soundlessly, urging him to stop, to let Joe come.

I could go to help him up, but I'm rooted to the spot, my feet are like lead and I'm sick to my stomach. This is the ghost of my past coming for me and I have no idea what to do. He makes his way over to me and holds his hand out. Is this my Ebenezer Scrooge moment? Is he going to take my hand and fly me back over my past, to that moment in time, to watch it as a spectator from above? To chastise me for the decisions I made in the past. It doesn't immediately register that that he is asking for the microphone until he's pulling it from my stiff, claw-like hand. My mouth is open. I'm gawping at him. This man is going to be my ruin.

I let him take the microphone.

CHAPTER EIGHTEEN: JONAH

To say the cacophony behind the door was horrific, would be an understatement of epic proportions. But there are no words to fully describe what it sounds like to hear a human being torn apart by a pack of monsters. It was so loud I wanted to scream to block out some of the sound. But I didn't. Maybe I owed it to him to listen to his final minutes. Maybe the shock had simply rooted me in place. I listened to every single second of the attack until the screams died away to nothingness. I listened until the scuffling of the creatures against the door stopped. I listened until the whole world was silent apart from the heavy breathing and choked tears within the foyer. I wished I hadn't. Keeping my head down, I couldn't look at any of the faces of the people in the coffee-shop, couldn't bear to see myself reflected back in their eyes as we listened to a man dying, a man who could have possibly been saved if I had just moved. I couldn't bare to see their hatred or recrimination.

When it was obvious that it was over I busied myself with getting the barricade back into place. My betrayal of Ross to save the rest of the group would be entirely pointless if inaction let the creatures inside to kill us regardless. I dragged the heavy pieces of wood, shuffling them slowly towards the door. Suddenly the load lightened considerably. Startled, I looked over to see Brad hefting the other end of the piece. He looked at me grimly but together we managed to get the barricade back into place. Finally the window was covered. I didn't know what would have been worse, seeing what remained of Ross on the other side of the door or seeing him getting up again to join the rest of the ravenous pack, bearing all of the wounds of his demise.

Once the barricade was back in place and we were sure it would hold, we made our way back up the stairs to the top level. I felt each step as I hefted myself upstairs. My everything hurt. Back in the main room we all avoided the table that had been occupied by Jake, Charlie and Ross only a short time ago. It didn't feel right to sweep aside their belongings, to disregard them that way.

Standing over the table, I had no idea what to say. It was too soon, too raw to eulogise them and it wouldn't have been right to do so in light of what happened. I didn't have the heart to continue to justify my position and why I hadn't let Ross back in and it no longer mattered anyway. He was dead. They were all dead. I didn't want to say that at least we were all alive. It felt callous even to think it, let alone to say it.

Clicking the TV back on, desperate for some noise in the quiet room, I went behind the counter to splash some cold water on my face from the tiny sink back there. I needed a minute, to gather myself. My nose wrinkled at the smell behind the counter, and it took a little while for my badly fuddled brain to work out the smell was me. Smelling was one of my pet hates but I had neither the energy nor the bravery to go to have a wash in the unisex bathrooms in the other room. It was much preferable to be stinking and together with the people who couldn't look me in the face than alone and vulnerable. At least we all stank. Cupping my hands under the meagre stream from the tap, I gulped at the pool in my dirty hands. It was nowhere near enough but it did a little to alleviate my hellishly dry mouth. I wondered if the sink was deep enough to drown myself in. I didn't think anyone else would mind, not by the atmosphere in the room or the feeling of their eyes boring into my back.

Filling the pitcher that was nestled under the sink, I left it on the counter in full view of everyone else to help themselves to. We didn't know if the water supply would stay on or for how long but as long as it remained we wouldn't die of thirst. The food situation was another thing altogether. Between us we had consumed a staggering amount of snacks. During the party atmosphere, before the boys went outside, no-one was thinking about the word 'ration'. But soon we were going to get hungry. The options seemed to be, either sit tight and hope the army got to us before we went all Uruguayan rugby team and ate each other, let the creatures go all Uruguayan rugby team and eat us or make our own bid for freedom. I turned up the TV, hoping for more information from the emergency broadcast. The fact it helped to dispel some of the heavy silence that was hanging over the group was a welcome side effect.

The broadcast had changed since we'd first turned it on yesterday. They were giving more detail on the situation but even so, it wasn't looking good. The outbreak had surged through the entirety of the city in a little over a day. Amsterdam was pretty much a no-go area and the army was sending more and more soldiers to man the barricades keeping the creatures from spilling into the surrounding towns, cities and countryside. They cut to scenes of the soldiers beating back hordes of the recently living from the saw-horses and concrete blocks they'd been using as roadblocks. My mouth instantly dried back up again. There seemed to be thousands of them. More were being added to their ranks every time the creatures bit someone and left enough of them intact for the reanimated body to get walking again. The army had their hands full trying to stop the spread. They hadn't even gone back into the city to do any search and rescue yet. They were advising anyone who could see the broadcast to sit tight and wait for them but they didn't give any time frames as to when that might be. Looking at the hoards surging forward at the barricades it was not beyond the realms of possibility that the time-frame could be weeks.

As I looked around the room, there was fear on every single one of the faces of the assembled motley crew. It was obvious from their expressions that they'd thought the same as me - we were going to be here for a while. There was definitely not enough food for those of us that were left for more than a couple of days. I didn't want to be the one to say it. I already felt like a grim reaper. Thankfully Tim, in his own way, saved me from having to say what everyone was thinking out loud.

"They're not coming for us are they? Oh God. Why did we eat all that fucking cheese last night?! Jesus Christ we ate all the cheese and now we're going to starve!" he wailed.

**

Until the words burbled up and out of me like an exceptionally fizzy burp I didn't know I was going to say anything. It was as mindless as shouting at the TV during a movie until I realise I am standing up in a room full of people and Amelia is trying to hold on to my arm, her face a myriad of questions. I'm so confused about Jennifer's account of what had happened to Ross and the others. I was waiting for the horror, for the heavy weight of the truth hitting the air like a bad odour.

Before I really know what I am doing and what it could ever hope to achieve, I am walking down the steps to the stage, the harsh whispers of Amelia calling my name getting further and further away. I look at Jennifer's sweaty face, seeing the fear in her eyes, and I am right back there in that heady coffee-shop arguing about whether or not we should let a man who was running for his life back into the building.

I put my hand out, silently asking for the microphone she is holding. Her face is a mask of panic and I can smell the sweat on her as I pull it out of her unyielding grasp. It's not the time for a

228

catch up and even if it was, what are we going to say to each other? How's your PTSD doing? Oh you know, I'm screaming a bit less in the night since my doctor upped the sedatives, but the crippling guilt is still making it hard to get off the sofa? You? She knows why I am standing in front of her on this stage. I'm the only other person here that knows that what she just said was a total and utter lie.

I realise now why I didn't keep in contact with her after the airport. Seeing her again is too intense, it's giving me a horrible case of déjà vu, like I could turn around and Ross would be standing right there, cocky grin on his face, thumbs in his belt loops, saying "All right Joe-Joe?" But its not all right, it is so far from all right. I hate confrontation, about as much as I hate public speaking, which makes this a double whammy of social anxiety. Nevertheless I can't let it go. He was an awful person but deserves the truth. I couldn't help him at the time but at least I can do this for him now. It has to count for something. Doesn't it?

I scan the audience to find Amelia, who looks about as shocked as Jennifer. Their expressions mirror one another. Focusing on Amelia alone, like it's just me and her together in the safety of our flat, entwined together in the refuge of our bed, I start to tell her everything that happened. The truth this time.

CHAPTER NINETEEN: JENNIFER

We ransacked all of the cupboards and piled all the available food, bottles of water and fizzy pop onto one of the tables. The offering was miniscule and consisted almost entirely of sugar. I never thought I'd be yearning for a green salad or a crisp, green apple but I'd eaten nothing but crap and caffeine for days. It was starting to affect me. My body was calling out for nutrients in the midst of its sugar crash. My temper, pretty short at the best of times, was perilously close to snapping all together. I was tired, hungry, sorry, sore and scared. The tiny pile of food did nothing to alleviate the panic that was galloping through the group, threatening to engulf us. You could smell it in the air, something acrid, like ozone after a thunder storm. It was heady, along with the stink of our collective bodies and the weed lingering in the air.

Each of us looked between the meagre pile of food and the other faces in the room. Someone had to say something. I was desperate to fill the silence, but the last time I had said something a man had died while we all stood-by and listened. The first thing I was going to say after that wasn't to inform a room full of people that if we stayed put we would probably die of starvation but the pressure of the unsaid words fizzed on my tongue.

The emergency broadcast was not helpful. It didn't offer a time-frame for resolution but simply to stay where we were, stay away from the windows, wait for rescue. My stomach rumbled mutinously. I sat down and rubbed at my face, feeling the stiff little hairs that had sprouted on my upper lip. My cosmetics bag was sitting in the bathroom in the hotel, my tweezers on the side of the sink. I was going to be doing a splendid Charlie Chaplin impression if we were going to be stuck here for many more days, perilously thin and sporting a thick black moustache. Thinking about Charlie Chaplin made me visualise popcorn, a thick slab of butter melting lasciviously through the kernels, making them hot and dense. My stomach gurgled more insistently, offended at the way my mind was teasing it with the thought of cinema snacks. I couldn't stand it any more. I decided to try a softer approach with the group.

"We're going to have to try to escape," I said.

The sentence sounded too loud in the silent room, bouncing off the walls. Everyone stared at me for an uncomfortably long time. It was a horrible sensation. It was the kind of staring that happens when you've got something wedged in-between your teeth or peeking out of one nostril and you've been chatting away to someone unselfconsciously for a long time. I wiped the back of my hand across my nose, hoping I didn't have something hanging out of it. My hand came back flaked with old blood, older makeup but thankfully nothing else.

"How do you suggest we do that?" Tommy asked me petulantly, hands on his hips, a dark look on his face.

I resisted the urge to turn his words on him, repeat them back in a high querulous tone like the mithering old woman he reminded me of. The urge to be mean, coiled like a snake in the back of my throat, poised to lash out. The temptation was great but it wouldn't help anything so I clamped my mouth around it.

"You saw the TV. There are plenty of soldiers at the blockades. If we can get to them then they can pick us up and get us out of here."

"Well what about...." he began before I cut him off with a disgusted noise and a raised hand.

"I'm not the fucking oracle here. I know as much as you do. But we're low on food so, we can sit here and do nothing or go out there and do something. Your choice."

My attempt at not going heavy handed or lashing out had not worked for very long. The metaphorical rope of my temper was pulled taught, fibres curling away as it frayed dangerously.

"What about a car?" said Brad, to no one in particular. When no answer was forthcoming he continued "If we could get hold of a car we could drive to one of these - " he gestures to the TV playing footage of the heavily manned roadblocks on a loop "and get out that way. Or even drive to the airport ourselves if we can."

I could have kissed Brad for actually coming up with a practical solution without a question at the end.

"So come on then, who can drive?" Michael said looking around, his gaze landing on me.

"I don't know why you're looking at me," I told him. "I grew up in London. I never learned how to drive." I pulled at the remains of my shirt, ripped and dappled in blood, but still obviously cheap. "Do I look rich enough to have a parking space in LONDON!" I chuckled. Several nonplussed faces looked back at me. I guess it was just one of those things you only discussed as a Londoner.

London properties with dedicated parking were as rare as hen's teeth. In one block of flats I'd lived in the parking situation was so dire people often did laps around the streets, stalking anyone who looked like they were walking back to their car so they could pounce on the vacancy. I watched one guy drive round and round the road we lived on for an hour, desperate to find a space and end his interminable commute. He got redder and redder on every lap. It had not convinced me to start to learn.

"Well I can drive," said Kate, putting her hand up tentatively. Smiles blossomed around the room. Someone else I could have kissed.

"We could steal a car, hot wire it and drive to the airport!" Ian said excitedly, definitely living his *Grand Theft Auto* fantasy.

"Do you know how to hot wire a car?" Joe asked.

"Well no. But I'm sure I could look it up on YouTube...oh. Well I'm sure it's not that diffi....." the rest of his sentence faded away in his mouth. He shut it with an audible clack, looking bereft.

At that moment, it seemed to hit all of us at once that we were not in an action movie. Nobody had an incredible set of skills or muscles piled on top of one another like scoops of ice-cream. This was real life. We were a small group of people with no, or unsatisfying careers, a healthy amount of personal debt and delusions of grandeur from too many Netflix shows where the protagonist defuses a bomb or lands a jet without having any previous experience. We were not mercenaries. I worked in marketing, and had to devise a trick, as a single woman, to be able to open particularly stubborn jars by breaking the seal with a teaspoon because my puny arms were just not up to the job. I wasn't going to be cracking skulls with my bare hands or doing nifty Kung Fu moves. We couldn't even Batman the situation with a load of tools. There was a bottle opener, a butter knife and a couple of lighters amongst the packaged stroopwafel and cans of coke. Hardly a well stocked utility belt. It was barely a picnic.

"Bikes" shouted Meg from the back of the room. She seemed as uncomfortable with everyone staring at her as I was. She didn't have any bogeys either. Lowering her gaze to the floor. "Sorry, that's probably stupid," she muttered to her shoes.

"No, it's really not," Brad said contemplatively. "They don't easily break down, they're quicker than walking and the city is literally teeming with them. I think it's a great idea Meg," he said to her bowed head. I could see her cheeks colouring from where I stood. Maybe this would be the weirdest meet cute that ever happened. What a story to tell the kids!

After yesterday's failed attempts I'd rather hoped that my bike riding days might have been behind me, but Brad's logic couldn't be faulted. It did seem to be our best option. We'd seen how fast those things were and we'd seen what happened when you tried to outrun them. Shaking my head, I tried to get rid of the memory of Ross's screams, desperately trying to think about something, anything else. I attempted to imagine the outside, the little I saw while running and what could be glimpsed out of small window in the door. Apart from crying, sweating and thinking I was going to die, there was a vague memory of running past a bike rack at the end of the street. If we could get there without alerting any of the creatures and get moving we might be able to make it. I looked down at my poor hands, studded with grit and raw, like a peppered steak. Suffice to say I wasn't looking forward to round two but equally we couldn't stay in the coffee-shop, waiting for death.

As a group, agreeing that using bikes to escape was the only unanimous decision we could make. From there on we couldn't agree to anything. We watched the emergency broadcast which looped over and over and over again after giving the main points – stay inside, help is coming, it might be a while, look here's the Army! The images, that we must have all seen a hundred times or more, switched between soldiers manning roadblocks, walking down streets littered with bodies and back again. All of us were tourists. We didn't really know the city, but it didn't stop us arguing over the location of all of the images. Have you ever watched a movie with someone who is adamant that it is set in a certain city and won't be dissuaded? You have to look it up to prove to them that, what they were convinced was a backstreet taverna in Rio de Janeiro that they'd been to in the nineties, was actually a cafe in Norwich? Everyone was convinced they knew the locations from each shot and, without the internet, there was no way to prove otherwise. It was like the eighties all over again, when you had to trust what someone told you implicitly, as it was incredibly hard to find out to the contrary. There were no index cards in the library to prove or disprove an urban legend that your auntie categorically thought was true.

"We went past that yesterday."

"That's obviously Centraal station. Look at the brickwork!"

"That soldier is on a boat, that's never the pavement. Look, it's moving!"

"Didn't you see that bus stop outside of the airport? It's obviously at the airport. It makes perfect sense the army would be based there."

Michael and Brad thought that the man on TV, that they had christened The Colonel, due to the plethora of stripes on his crumpled uniform, was speaking outside of the airport. They wanted to take bikes from the rack outside and cycle directly to the airport itself. They tried desperately to convince the rest of us that a nine mile bike ride, in the middle of the apocalypse would be easy as cake. I wondered if either of them had ridden a bike recently or indeed ridden a bike at the fastest possible speed they could manage for nine miles.

A couple of years ago, I'd had the unfortunate experience of attending a spin class, in yet another vain attempt to get fit. I thought the two things were probably comparable. Both included pushing your legs as fast as humanly possible while someone screamed at you. The bikes didn't have mileometers on them but I was reasonably sure the distance covered in that hellish class was nowhere near nine miles. Even so I'd practically fallen from the saddle of the bike, wondering why my entire undercarriage had gone numb as I took my first wobbly steps onto solid ground, drenched in sweat and breathing like an asthmatic donkey. That had been bad but my experience with a real bike had been even worse and was painfully evident in my now disgusting, weeping hands. If the creatures were here to stay someone would probably make a fortune inventing an exercise class combining spin and survival. I didn't particularly fancy being the beta tester for that particular experiment.

Meg and Kate wanted to go to Centraal station. They thought it made the most sense that the biggest train station in the city was bound to have some kind of army presence. But I was sceptical. We could travel back to the station and find it overwhelmed with the monsters, then we could be trapped underground with no way out while the things picked us off one by one. In the dark, lonely confines of the station. I didn't want to be running through a train tunnel in the pitch black, nowhere to go but forward as I was run down like a dog. The very thought of it sent my claustrophobia into overdrive.

Personally, I was convinced one of the shots was of a soldier on a boat. I tried to tell the group, many of whom had splintered off into twos and threes to yell at one another about their own preferred plan, about the canal where I had first seen the creatures. I wanted to tell them that until the pyramid had become too tall and until they had pulled the first bystander down with them, the canal's sides had been doing a pretty good job at keeping the creatures contained. The vertical, slippery stone made it difficult for them to gain purchase and certainly to gain much speed. I tried to tell the group that if the army were using boats that it was more than likely they had stationed themselves at the ferry passenger terminal, as it would be easier to defend with water on all sides. To me it made perfect sense.

Everyone was an expert and no-one could agree with anybody else. We needed to come to a decision. Someone had to acquiesce so we could decide on which location we were going to start moving towards. We couldn't be in all places at once and no-one wanted to split up. I thought I could probably get the girls on side. Centraal station was at least close to the ferry terminal. If we made our way to the terminal and it was a bust then it was less than a mile to get to the station. Though I'm sure half a mile when you're running for your life felt more like a marathon than jaunty stroll.

The boys would be harder to convince since the airport was in entirely the other direction. Some of the group like Tommy, Tim, Ian and John hadn't seemed to have made their minds up completely about the best place to head out to. Maybe I could get them to see things my way, using my powers of persuasion. The marketing profession, where I worked, was essentially just being able to convince a consumer, beyond a shadow of doubt, that their lives would be immeasurably better should they buy the newest phone/perfume/handbag etc. Now I just had to use those skills to convince the rest of the group to go where I thought we needed to go.

Speaking to the group in pairs and singles, I cajoled and explained, nudging as many people as I could towards my way of thinking. Making ardent eye contact and listening hard to them I worked the room as hard as any networking event with a big client that needed to be wooed. It didn't matter that I was more used to schmoozing over a Danish pastry and coffee in my best suit rather than with one eye swollen shut over a mountain of junk food in a boarded up coffee-shop. The concept was the same.

I managed to convince Tommy, John, Ian, Joe and more reluctantly Kate that it was definitely the ferry terminal in the footage, reasoning that even if it wasn't, it would be a good place to defend ourselves while we decided on our next moves. I was pretty sure that my plan would be the majority vote should it come to it. "Girl's still got it" I thought. My hubris was nearly our undoing.

**

I am half right. There is a ghost of Christmas past in the room, but it's not Joe, it's Ross. When Joe gets onto the stage, all I can see is Ross's face as he began his run back to the perceived safety behind that closed door. It is reflected in Joe's eyes. He is here to punish me for my lie, and I deserve it. He is the one person who truly understands. I give up the microphone to him and watch him weigh it in his hands like it is a bomb. The truth of his revelations could blow up my life. And his. I can see he understands that in the way he licks his lips, the way his eyes dart around the faces watching him. A mean little part of me is glad. It's not as easy as it looks and if he wants to press the detonator he needs to understand the enormity of it. I've passed the microphone on to him like a baton. I wonder what he is going to do with it.

Tremulously he introduces himself into the microphone, his first words spoken too close so the PA system reverberates sharply, making everyone put their hands to their ears. I see his eyes zero in on a pretty woman sitting in the seat next to the empty one he must have just vacated. Finding her face in the crowd seems to give him strength. I am a little jealous. He begins to speak.

"Hello everyone. My name is Jonah," My head whips round from the audience to stare at him. He looks me in the eyes and I feel like I don't even know him. "Joe. Everyone calls me Joe. I am the Joe from Jennifer's story and I want to clear a few things up." I close my eyes as he begins.

CHAPTER TWENTY: JONAH

To give Jennifer her due, she was pretty slick in her ability to sell her idea as the best one. It was evident why it was her day job. She would have been able to sell salt to a slug, as my dad used to say. I didn't need much convincing. Like the others, I had watched the emergency broadcast over and over, but each picture moved too quick for me to be entirely convinced where any of the sites truly were. They could have been right outside the front door for all I knew. I was happy enough for someone else to take the lead, having lost any taste I might have had for making the big decisions. The decisions I had made had led to people dying, Ross most certainly, but possibly Keith too. I was more than happy to take a back seat now. The others seemed to acquiesce to Jennifer as well, even those like Michael and Brad who were convinced otherwise seemed to begrudgingly agree to let her take the reins on this decision. It was too hard to resist giving up the responsibility for everyone present.

The plan was to go to the bike rack outside, grab a bike each and follow the canal along to the ferry passenger terminal and hopefully to rescue. Jennifer assured us that keeping the water to one side would be safer. She was convinced that we'd get to the terminal and be able to throw ourselves on the mercy of the Army. What happened after that point she was vague on. None of us knew what the army would do when we got there, they had after all told us to keep inside and await rescue. This was completely the opposite. They could take us in, give us a hot drink and get us to safety before allowing us to fly home to our loved ones. On the other hand we had no real way of knowing whether they would just shoot us on site, not leaving anything to chance with a rampant contagion in the city. I suspect that Jennifer had thought of that possibility as well. Her eyes went shifty whenever someone discussed what the army would do with us. She was a great salesperson, but I would imagine a crap poker player with such an obvious tell. Still, it was much better than anything I had come up with – the frontrunner currently being wait for it all to be over and try not to cry.

"Brad. We're going to have to get those boards off and see if we can have a look," I called over to him.

He nodded grimly and followed me down the stairs. We moved the boards away from the door and tried peering through the sliver of window. I could see the sky, the canal, the bike rack and a few feet of pavement streaked with blood. It didn't give us a lot of information. For all we knew, a hoard of them could be standing by the side of the door, shushing each other and waiting for us to come out. I doubted it very much, as the creatures didn't seem to have much cognitive reasoning, but there was no way to really be absolutely, one hundred percent sure. Putting my ear against the heavy door, the only sound was the distant whooshing of the wind, like putting your ear against a shell at the beach. I couldn't hear anything else, not plotting or planning, no sounds other than the wind and a few lone seagulls. For such a bustling city to be so silent was terrifying. I was not filled with confidence.

Looking back at the assembled group, depleted and nervous and waiting for me to tell them if it was alright to open the door. I didn't know. I shrugged miserably at them. Jennifer came to stand next to me to crane her neck in the tiny window, bobbing around like a bird trying to see something I might have missed. She leaned her forehead against the window, leaving a smear across the glass. Her chin wobbled.

"I just don't know," I whispered to her. "Should we?"

A tear slipped underneath her swollen eye, tracking a path down her dirty face. She took a deep shuddering breath and tried to grasp my hand. I tried my best not to cringe at the feeling of macerated meat against my skin and gave it a little squeeze, hoping I wasn't hurting her. Without a word she opened her good eye and turned to the group.

"So? Let's do this," she said with artificial sunshine in her voice.

We packed the remaining food and drink into whatever receptacles we could find. My backpack was perilously full so I stuffed two cans of coke into my trouser pockets. My bulging hips made me look like an extra in a Western, ready to pull two pistols out for a shoot-out in a saloon. It made me remember Ross asking if we needed to take supplies when we left the cheese shop, My heart contracted painfully in my chest. I put the rest of his things in a carrier bag I'd found under the sink - maybe I could give them to his girlfriend if we ever got home. Though how I would look her in the face when giving her back her dead boyfriend's wallet, knowing I had stood between him and safety, was beyond me. That was a future problem and I tried to put it to the back of my mind. There were more pressing issues at hand. Maybe, I thought darkly, if I were lucky I wouldn't make it back and wouldn't have to face her at all. Amelia's face loomed large in my mind. She wouldn't feel lucky if I never returned. I had to try to make it back for her.

Physically leaving the coffee-shop was harder than I thought it would be. It had become familiar and felt safe. The urge to put the barricade back in place, go back upstairs and sit down on one of the banquettes was almost physical. I could rip open a packet of stroopwawfel, and refuse to move, like a toddler having a tantrum. I didn't want to venture into the cold, silent street to face the unknown. The words "Let's just stay" were quivering on my lips. Watching the others pack up our meagre belongings, I let the words die in my mouth. A people pleaser to the end. At least I hoped it wasn't the end.

The air outside was cold, the wind whipping around my ankles and prying under my jacket and shirt with its icy fingers. No creatures lingered at the side of the door, waiting to catch us out. The street was empty. Creepily quiet. Just the sound of the wind and the mournful cries of the seagulls, diving and swooping to snaffle up titbits, the origin of which I didn't want to consider. We left the building en masse, forming a tight circle around one another and shuffling out into the open. I have never felt so exposed and vulnerable before or since. All of my nerve endings jangled and sang like wind chimes. We shuffled along at an awkward pace, not wanting to run and draw attention, not wanting to go too slow and get caught out. Beside me Kate started to cry, quietly at first but slowly gathering in intensity. Her sobs jiggled against my arm, her sniffling was loud in my ear.

"We should go back," she whispered wetly. No one responded to her. "We should go back. NOW!" she said louder still.

I looked over at her desperately, trying to silently communicate with her. Trying to get her to shut up. Her eyes were shut tight, streaming profusely to mix with her equally leaking nose. She couldn't see my silent urging. I had no choice but to use my words.

"Please," I whispered back to her. "Please. Stop." But she couldn't. I could see it in her shuddering shoulders, in her face clenched in like a walnut. Like me she was fighting the animal urge to run back to a safe burrow, to climb under the table, in a room with central heating, electric lighting and barricaded doors. Safe. Before I could say anything else she unlinked her arm from Ian's and mine. I reached for her but felt the fabric of her jacket slipping through my fingers like sand.

Kate ran back to the open mouth of the door. Each slap of her feet on the pavement sounded like a gunshot in the silent street. I gawked stupidly as she disappeared back inside, slamming the door shut behind her. How could this be happening? I looked to my right, hoping it was a stress induced hallucination and that she'd be staring at me, wondering why I was no longer walking forward. I turned. She wasn't there. The rest of the group are stared at the gap she had left, as shocked as me. Looking at the, now closed, door I considered joining her, back into the dark burrow of the coffee-shop. Better to be hungry for a little while than a meal for something else. I might have done it if the sound of them coming hadn't broken through my reverie. There was no time for rational decision making. We had to get out of there.

The group broke apart, scattering like a piece of porcelain hit with a hammer. We were no longer united with linked arms, stoicism and a plan. Instead we were reduced to the proverbial chickens without heads, running away from the sound of impending death, clucking wildly. I ran towards the bikes, keeping them in focus and pumping my arms and legs as hard as possible. I had no other aim than to reach them, to get far away from the creatures.

The world was a cacophonous crescendo of noise behind me, snarling and snapping and thunderous footsteps. Grabbing the nearest bike in the rack, I pulled the heavy contraption out of the mechanism and swung my leg over, pushing off as hard and swiftly as I could muster. The wind whipped the tears out of my eyes. I was free. I had to restrain myself from whooping in delight.

My glee was short lived. From behind me was the sound of Stuart's scream. Whirling around on the uncomfortable seat, I tried to see him in the melee. He was so close to the bike rack but one of the creatures had latched on to him before he'd managed to grab a bike. Ross. Or the thing that had once been Ross but was now something other and something less at the same time. His grin was now pulled up and out on one side, a red gash along his cheek to his temple, like a nightmare clown. One of his eyes had spilled down his cheek and swung with every snapping turn of his head. I could see his jaw working as he grabbed and pulled at Stuart, teeth clashing down on one another, miming what they would do once they got Stuart's flesh between them. His shirt was stuck to his body with blood, the clinging fabric pooling into his concave stomach. The creatures that had killed him had obviously left with most, if not all, of Ross's innards. It didn't seem to slow him down. He grappled and thrashed with Stuart who desperately tried to fight him off. He was shrieking Ross's name over and over into his face, hoping he might recognise him as a friend rather than a tasty morsel. It didn't seem to be working. The Ross-thing snapped and snarled, tearing at Stuart with mindless ferocity.

I stopped and dropped the bike, fully intending

to get back to Stuart, to help him. But before I'd taken a step towards him the Ross-thing managed to snag Stuart's hand with the side of his gaping mouth, crunching into his fingers. They scattered over the floor like a dropped tray of cocktail sausages. Stuart grabbed at his missing fingers, allowing Ross to surge forward, pulling Stuart to him in a deathly embrace. Ross nuzzled his mangled face in to Stuart's neck, clamping down on his throat and shaking like a terrier with a rat. Stuart's screams turned to bloody gurgles as he began to drown in his own blood. There was nothing I could do. It was too late.

Turning back to my discarded bike I threw myself onto the hard saddle, feeling the painful reverberation in my crotch, radiating into my stomach. There was no time to even register the agony of my bruised testicles. Stopping to cup my aching groin would probably ensure I lost both balls, and my life, to Ross or one of his cannibalistic friends. There would be time to cry for Stuart later, to mourn that I had truly lost him completely to Ross after all.

Tommy and John streaked past me the other way, calling out to Stuart. I was too far away to try to grab for either of them. Soon their screaming mixed with the moans and shrieks of the dead, and the nearly dead. I didn't turn round but kept peddling.

So much for no man left behind. I pushed hard to catch up with the rest of the group.

******

The phrase 'a deer in the headlights' now makes sense to me. I'm frozen to the spot. All I can do it try to keep my eyes trained on Amelia, but the footlights shining into my eyes and kicking out an immense heat, has rendered me a blithering idiot. My mouth is sticky from fear, cheap whiskey and untold truths. I wipe the corners of my lips with my fingertips and rub them on my jeans. Amelia can see me floundering. She stands up, cupping her hands around her mouth and shouts down to me.

"Tell us what happened!"

The guy in front of her looks around, offended by her loud yell in his ear. She sticks her tongue out at him and crosses her eyes, daring him to say something. I smother a laugh. She always knows what to say. Her confidence emboldens me.

"Go on Joe," Jennifer whispers beside me, putting her hand on my shoulder. It's rough. I look at the scars on her palm as she pulls it away, and stuffs it into the pocket of her suit trousers.

She sits on the chair and takes a long swallow from the glass on the table in front of her, her throat bobbing as she glugs the liquid. She wipes her mouth with the back of her hand and I can see her sitting behind the counter of the cheese shop with us, slugging at the bottle of water from my backpack. The ghosts of Ross and Stuart leer over her shoulder. A trick of the footlights. I think I know why she told their stories the way she did. It doesn't feel like a lie any more. It seems more like compassion. Nobody needs to be freely given the intimate details of their last moments, no-one else needs their ghosts to follow them like they follow us. I understand now.

CHAPTER TWENTY-ONE: JENNIFER

Our little group had shrunk significantly, having lost Kate to the confines of the coffee-shop and with Tommy, John and Stuart fallen to the monsters, we cut a lonely sight, cycling down the pavement towards the ferry terminal. We passed the aftermath of what seemed to be several skirmishes, but saw no other living people. We could have been the last people left alive in the city. The light was starting to fail and the impending sunset was beautiful. It was the kind of sunset you take a picture of and upload with something flippant like #travellife #sunsetview #sorrynotsorry! to Instagram. It made me want to take my useless phone out of my pocket and hurl it into the water, sickened that I'd once been so vacuous but simultaneously so jealous of that past me. Past me would probably have been taking selfies with a glass of ouzo right about now, if I'd booked a Greek island instead of Amsterdam. She definitely wouldn't have been trying to hold on to a bike handle with shredded hands and trying to keep an eye out for the reanimated dead.

We peddled along silently, dodging bodies and body parts until we could see the ferry terminal in the distance. It was easy to spot; a large glass structure in the shape of a wave. Each glass panel glinted in the dying sun, like a many eyed insect. Rearing up beside it was a docked cruise ship, with its own abundance of glinting glass windows, many storeys high. I couldn't see a soul onboard. There was no-one hanging over any of the balconies waving to us like my first day in Amsterdam from the tourists on boat tours. That didn't mean there was nobody actually aboard. Maybe they'd been told to all get away from the windows for safety. Maybe somewhere deep inside the ship all of the passengers were inside the ballroom trying to keep themselves entertained with talent acts, or beat poetry, or improvised acid jazz. For all we knew Derek, retired from Hull, could be wowing his fellow passengers with his majestic fire poi skills, or ability to throw his voice into a creepy ventriloquist's dummy that he'd brought onboard. Much to the chagrin of his long suffering wife Doreen. On the other hand, if one of the infected had gotten aboard, that same ballroom could be full of the chewed remains of Derek, Doreen, his fellow passengers and a few of the infected waiting for a delivery of fresh flesh.

We would have to make our way past the ship if we were going to get to the terminal and ascertain whether the blockade from the broadcast was there. But I had a sinking feeling it wasn't going to be. Everything looked a little different, more than a little unfamiliar. None of the landmarks from the broadcast were evident. My gut clenched. I was wrong. I had made a terrible mistake. Oh shit. I had to try not to panic and instead needed to scrabble around for a plan, some way of fixing the terrible mistake I'd made. The only choices were either pushing on blithely and seeing what happened or turning to the group, made smaller by my decision to leave, and fess up to my almost confirmed suspicion. The heat of shame and embarrassment rushed up my neck and into my face, pushing hot tears of frustration from my eyes. I had done what I thought was right and now it might come to literally bite me in the arse. I wanted to scream and throw myself on the ground, thumping my fists on the floor. It wasn't fair. Why me?

Pushing on wasn't an option, not suspecting what I did. It wasn't right and I might end up killing yet more people if I did so. Stopping and turning around to the little group, more than a few with tears in their own eyes, I opened my mouth. Nothing came out. I didn't know how to begin.

"It's not the right place is it?" asked Meg in a small voice. She didn't sound mad, which made it worse, like when your parents tells you they're not angry, just disappointed. It stung, shaming me further. It would be vastly preferable for there be shouting and recriminations rather than the tired, sad sound of Meg's voice asking whether I'd stubbornly rowed them up shit creek and thrown the paddles overboard without a second thought because of my over-confidence.

"We're here now. We might as well have a look," she said to me gently. I nodded mutely, thinking I would probably start bawling if I opened my mouth again.

We made our way to the building, peddling slowly past the huge cruise ship to get to the entrance. Surely if the army were here someone would have stopped us by now, but it was too quiet. The only sounds were the turning of our wheels, the wind and screaming in the distance. I hoped it was seagulls but wasn't all together confident. We dismounted outside the glass building. Inside was a wide, browning streak of blood on the floor, like someone had been dragged away as they bled profusely. There was a single shoe on the ground. Tickets and trash swirled lightly in the December breeze. Small porcelain and plastic trinkets lay shattered from a toppled table in the souvenir shop. A dark plume of smoke was starting to leak from the sandwich shop within as an oven timer chirped shrilly into the silence. I shivered, as much from the shock as the cold. I'd made a bad call. Again. There was so much blood on my hands, both literal and figurative. I turned round to speak to the rest of the group, to ask them whether they thought we should go to the train station, when I saw the first figure making their way down the gang plank of the cruise ship. The words shrivelled up in my mouth, puckering my lips like sour fruit.

**

Sitting down on the chair left for me by the sound engineer I take a long swallow of the water, not realising how thirsty all of the confiding had made me, and return it to the table. Looking down into my lap, I see the cratered, pitted surface of my palms. There are dark circles around Joe's eyes and his hand shakes a little when he reached for the microphone. We both carry our scars from our time out there. Both seen and unseen. I close my eyes and wait for him to start speaking, waiting for the truth to come tumbling out of his mouth, to bury us both in an avalanche of guilt. He clears his throat. His feet shuffle a little bit on the wooden stage. I hear the cry from his girlfriend in the audience. He starts to speak.

"We lost a lot of people in Amsterdam. What Jennifer has said is true but....." I hear some burbles from the crowd, wondering why this man has taken over the microphone if he truly has no objection to my story so far.

259

"What in the holy mansplaining is this?!" a woman calls out from the audience. It makes me smile.

I open my eyes to see how uncomfortable Joe is on the stage. He's shuffling from foot to foot like he needs to pee. I decide to put him out of his misery.

"Tell them how we got out. Tell them how we're here. Explain how we survived to tell them this story," I say to him gently.

He clears his throat again and begins. Leaning back in my chair I let it all play out behind my eyelids like a projected film.

CHAPTER TWENTY-TWO: KEITH

I enjoyed the Saturday kick-about with the lads but didn't take it too seriously. It was obvious that there wasn't going to be a talent scout waiting in the wings to take one of us to live out our fantasy in Wembley Stadium. We were far too old. Our school days were a long time behind us. You wouldn't know that, watching some of these guys, pounding up the field and slide tackling each other with abandon. It made me wince. I was definitely too old to be hobbling around on crutches with a broken ankle or a torn ligament. The boys took every win or defeat like it was the difference between relegation or winning the Champions League. I watched it all from my vantage point, waiting around in the goal mouth for the action to get to my end of the pitch. I was always the goalie. It meant not having to slog up and down the field for ninety minutes and I usually just had to stick my hand out to let the ball ricochet away.

We'd played football pretty much every weekend, since we were little lads. It was almost a force of habit. I kept playing to have a laugh and as a (losing) battle against my weight. Before Tony told everyone he wouldn't be playing any more because of his knees, he had sidled up to me at the bar one Saturday night and admitted that of course he knees were a problem but a larger part was that he just couldn't be doing with the drama any longer. In the bastardised words of Roger Murtaugh from *Lethal Weapon*; he was just too old for that shit. I was starting to agree but my rapidly expanding waistline didn't. But he had put the idea in my head.

I'd been a very fit young man, able to eat like a horse, with a metabolism that seemed to burn the calories off before I'd even finished consuming them. I'd scoffed at my dad when he told me it wouldn't last. My dad was a large man with a big belly that, when I'd been younger and slimmer, had thought was entirely his fault. Purely a lack of self control. With the arrogance of youth I didn't think that perhaps the same fate was written for me somewhere deep in my genes just stealthily biding its time. I thought I'd be a svelte lady-killer for ever, but the beer, kebabs and sedentary life style took their toll. As soon as the clock ticked round to my thirtieth birthday my metabolism hit the skids. I had only to look at a pie and it might as well have been sellotaped to my middle. Not that it stopped me eating the pie though.

By my mid thirties I was sporting the exact same kind of belly my dad had carried. It was identical to the one he was wearing when he died from a heart attack in his fifties. It was like permanently wearing a solid sack of sand on the front of my body with no ability to take it off or get any kind of relief. It made me feel like an old man and played havoc with my back. My knees hurt all the time and I was likely to put out my neck if I dared to sleep funny or sneeze the wrong way. It was making me nervous. I didn't want to go out the same way as dad but was at a loss on how to go about making changes.

My job was pretty sedentary. My morning commute was an hour of sitting on a train. Then sitting in my office chair for eight hours, in between trips to the kitchen for a brew and out to Subway at lunchtime for a twelve inch meatball marinara. On Friday nights the whole office went for drinks, a send off for another shitty week. I'd end each working day by sitting on the train for the journey home, followed by an evening of sitting on the sofa. At my last check up my doctor told me I was pre-diabetic and had a high enough blood pressure to make him nervous. I left with a prescription and a bee in my ear about getting some more exercise.

Of course it was obvious that I needed to work out more but not only was it uncomfortable to do so, I was considering leaving the team too. Giving up the position of goalie was out of the question, it suited me down to the ground. I wasn't fit enough to leave my position and run the length of the pitch every week. Any lunge or dive for the ball left me huffing and puffing, holding onto the bar to get my breath back. Standing in goal, yelling at the strikers, giving them my encouragement or berating the referee worked just fine for me, even so, I felt my age every Saturday afternoon.

Between the physical fatigue and the drama between Joe, Ross and Stuart my commitment was starting to waver. Every Saturday was like being in the middle of a lover's triangle and I was considering just getting a swim membership. It would be a lot more gentle on my joints for one thing. Would I have to admit I was no longer a young pup if I gave up football and spent my Saturday mornings in the slow lane with the nattering blue rinse ladies? Probably. I wasn't quite ready to do that yet and I'd miss going out to the pub after the games and having a laugh with my mates, when they weren't all bickering and vying for each other's attention that is.

Joe's face was a sight to behold when Ross announced he was going to be Stuart's best man, and would be organising the stag do, not Joe. I felt bad for him but a couple of us did wonder, on the walk to the bus stop that week, whether Joe would even come at all, and if he did whether he'd have a sour puss on him all weekend like that night at the pub. Tommy, John and I even took a bet on it, only something friendly. One thing was for sure; there would definitely be some fireworks over the decision.

In the next couple of weeks the tension was palpable. Joe and Ross would spat and bicker every time they were together, after every game and at the pub. The group WhatsApp chat had become incredibly awkward. Each time Joe put forward a suggestion, which would inevitably be the antithesis of the trip Ross was obviously trying to plan, I could feel myself cringe. I tried my best to ignore it, to go with the flow and look forward.

It had been ages since I'd been on holiday and I was well up for this one. The organising of the trip was for me, at least, pretty stress free, having only myself to please. There was no wife or girlfriend in the picture to be annoyed at my choice of destination. As a younger man, I'd always been quite popular with the ladies but since piling on the weight my confidence had taken a hit. I hadn't had a girlfriend for some time. I'd considered dating apps but didn't want to have to go through the highs and lows of booking dates and then having them fall through once the girl saw me up close and personal. As such, I wasn't averse to the thought of buying a little company in the red light district. It had been a while, and I knew as long as I had the cash then I wouldn't be turned down for a date, even if it was only a transactional, one-sided affair.

Everything was fine until we boarded the plane and took our seats. The seat itself was snug and the seatbelt was more of a struggle than I remembered. I desperately tried to hide it from the rest of the lads. There was no way I was going to ask for a seatbelt extender from the flight attendant. Surely I wasn't there yet? I managed to clip the contraption together under the heft of my gut but it was a close call. I was a little jealous of Jonah's shirt. At least his wasn't threatening to roll up like a Venetian blind like mine was.

I'm ashamed to say that the leering and the banter got away from me a little when seeing those sex workers lining the streets in their little glass rooms. I didn't act my best or my most chivalrous. We had been drinking solidly for hours at that point. I'm not making excuses. But maybe I am. When Jonah suggested we head on to the theatre I wasn't disappointed, thinking it was just an aperitif before we got to the brothels, a sex livener if you will. Suffice to say it was very different to the way strip clubs are portrayed in the movies. It wasn't glamorous or sexy, instead it felt seedy and far too intimate. It hit home pretty quickly that these were real women, and seeing them up close and personal in the light of day sobered me up quickly. The woman who danced for me looked bored. She might as well have been filling in her tax return for all of the enjoyment on her face. It was just a job for her, and the moves she made looked more like muscle memory than actual enjoyment. I felt horribly awkward and unable to work out what to do with my face or my hands. Was I meant to be smiling? Trying to look sexy? Was I meant to stay silent or to call out encouragement? I almost gave her a thumbs up at one point. The whole thing felt like a minefield that I had no idea how to navigate. It was certainly not floating my boat in any way. I was desperate for it to end.

I had been so focused on not doing anything weird with my face and not looking like a big sweaty perv that the alarm from my phone almost made me jump out of my skin. Looking around wildly, I hoped it hadn't been triggered by something I had done. My hands, laying limply in my lap, didn't look as thought they had taken on a mind of their own and grabbed a woman without me noticing. There were so many signs, in different languages, telling you to basically keep your hands to yourself. All looky, no touchy. Or else. It didn't seem to be beyond the realms of possibility that there would be a reprimanding alarm should you break, what seemed to be, the joint's cardinal rule. There were plenty of bouncers floating around the room to really drive that point home too. Nothing sexier than looking up from a gyrating woman to see a bald bloke built like a brick shithouse staring at you intently. I felt that if one of my, or my fellow audience member's hands, were to leave their laps, then they'd be snapped off like a dry twig, very quickly, by one of the walking monoliths dressed in the usual uniform of bouncers; all black, too tight t-shirts (to show off those well honed muscles), plastic armbands and scowls. It took me longer than I'd like to admit to realise it was not a bad behaviour alarm but my own phone making the loud, monotonous blare. The realisation was almost a relief. Everyone, including the strippers who all stopped what they were doing, stared down intently at their phones. It meant the woman I had given my money to wouldn't have to finish her set and I wouldn't have to worry about doing anything weird like inadvertently licking my lips when she took her top off. More relief.

The feeling of relief disappeared when I actually looked at the message on my phone. After drinking so much in the day I need to close one eye to read it properly, but even when the words stopped swimming enough for me to read them it still didn't make sense. Threat to life? I looked up, desperate for some clarification. All the other punters looked as equally confused as me. It was probably the only time that it is acceptable to look at another man getting a lap dance, without worrying about getting a slap for your troubles.

Any positive feelings went flying out of the window altogether when Joe came bounding up the stairs to find me. He wasn't so good at keeping his feelings off his face and now he looked absolutely terrified. Something that did not fill me with confidence. Joe was fit and all muscle too. He looked like someone who could handle himself. He told me that they were going to leave and see what was going on. Not only did I think that was a terrible plan any way the fact that someone like Joe was scared made me sure I really would have no chance out there.

Looking around the room at the plush sofas, bottles of champagne and beautiful women, I just couldn't see the impetus to leave. Even if it were a nuclear strike the idea of being sat on my arse while it happened was much preferable. Better that than heaving and wheezing to save my life. As much as I disliked physical exertion it paled in comparison to how much I hated being scared. I never watched horror movies and couldn't abide jump scares, shock pranks or anything that was going to make my poor heart thump in my chest. It made me think of my dad and panic. I always had my hands over my eyes at the part when the good guys are walking down a dark corridor, or edging their way to freedom and you just know something is going to pop out and grab them. If that happened to me, in the real world, then I wouldn't be able to run or

269

fight or win. I would simply lie down in the street and die. I didn't have it in me to be one of the heroes, battling to survive. I was tired and unfit and if something chased after me I'd probably just let it win to avoid the cardio.

I know he didn't want to leave me there and I appreciated his concern but I am a grown man and able to come to my own decisions and conclusions The plan didn't seem a strong one, wandering the streets without a clue didn't strike me as the best move to make. Plus I'd already got a blister from all the walking I'd done so far this weekend and my lower back ached something rotten. I waved him off, telling him I'd be fine but fear swelled in my chest like particularly bad heartburn. An altogether too familiar feeling. I didn't see the others, assuming they'd just left with Joe. Rather them than me I muttered quietly to myself a couple of times, trying to make myself feel more confident. I didn't know if it was the right decision but it was done now and there was no way I was going to try and find them all on the street.

The room was quiet pandemonium. The women milled around, robes hastily thrown over various states of undress. The men either raced down the stairs and out into the street or dithered in the lobby, not knowing what to do. In the middle of it, like the calm centre of a storm but feeling anything but, I sat on one of the leather sofas. I put my feet up on the table, saw them cresting over the hill of my belly, and waited. Soon I was joined by more and more men who obviously didn't know what else to do either. We sat on the array of sofas, making the room resemble the waiting area in a women's clothing department, a troupe of men lingering indefinitely. The main doors downstairs slammed shut, and a crescendo of banging and hammering commenced as the bouncers secured them. It seemed I had really sealed my fate. There was no leaving now unless I threw myself out of a window and scaled a drainpipe, or something equally unfeasible. The situation must be pretty serious if they were barricading us inside without a heads up. Everyone looked around at one another, eyebrows raised, communicating their fear telepathically. The room felt drenched in it, vying for prominence alongside the perfume and cologne of the assembled men and women.

Finally, after the banging was finished, a small group of bouncers came back into the main room. At their head was a sweaty man in an expensive looking suit. No matter how dapper the outfit it didn't detract from the awful syrup which was sliding around on his head from the increasing perspiration.

"Gentlemen," he said, taking a pause to wipe his

face with a silk handkerchief, knocking his wig even more askew.

"There is nothing to concern yourself about," he said, his eyes bulging out of his clammy face, belying the feeling behind his smooth words.

"We have closed the doors for your safety, and we ask that you stay here until we receive more information about the situation. To compensate you for the inconvenience, all champagne will be free for the next two hours and all dances will be half price for this time also."

A collective cheer went up from the men in the room. Free plonk and cheap dances seemed to be enough to quell the fear of the punters. From across the room I spied a couple of the women rolling their eyes at one another, obviously not pleased at the drop in earnings and not looking forward to the potentially sloppy attitude free drinks and fear were going to bring their way.

I didn't fancy another dance, feeling too antsy and awkward to even attempt faking enjoyment to the strippers gyrating while the world might be ending outside. The music had been turned way up against whatever noises might assault us from the outside, and my head was starting to pound. Having had enough practice in day drinking to know the only way out was through, I made my way to the bar, intent on being the first in line for the free champagne. The barman didn't see me. He and a bouncer had their heads pressed together to mitigate against the now banging music. Their conversation looked tense and unease settled deeper in my stomach. I wondered if the management were plying us with booze and boobs to keep us docile, a lot like the feeding and watering schedules on long haul flights, used to keep passengers dozy. The barman finally noticed me and slid the sweating bottle of champagne across the bar, in a gesture very close to utter dismissal. I understood I wasn't wanted and took the heavy bottle back to the sofa.

The free booze began to flow like a faucet. Soon there were empty bottles on every conceivable surface; down the sides of sofas, upside down in cooling buckets or on their sides, leaking pale liquid into the carpet. It was a concept that was obviously going down well. Maybe a little too well. It also seemed to be having the opposite effect to what management had planned. The men were not becoming subdued but rather riled up. Voices were rising against the steady thump of the music. Across the room two men square up to one another, one obviously not wanting to wait his turn for a half price dance. The atmosphere was turning sour and I wished I had gone with Joe and the rest of the boys, rather than staying here with a group of increasingly drunk, angry, horny dudes.

The dancers also sensed the barometric pressure change in the room. Not many of them were providing the half price dances they'd been roped into against their will by the sweaty management. I didn't blame them. I wasn't comfortable even being in the same room as a lot of these men, let alone taking my clothes off in front of them. Though they'd probably not be baying for that kind of dance, a fat man in skanky drawers being, probably a more niche market.

Returning to the bar, I stood next to the bouncer. He sat, staring at the gouges and stains in the top of the counter, rubbing the coarse stubble of his shaved head back and forth monotonously and self soothingly. He was obviously too engaged in his own thoughts to notice me. I collected another bottle of champagne and waggled it at him in the international gesture for "Want one?". He looked at it thoughtfully, seemingly deciding whether or not to refuse alcohol while at work. Shrugging to himself the bouncer poured a glass and knocked back the liquid in one. He burped loudly and unashamedly before taking another bottle from the generous collection on the bar.

"Not meant to drink on the job," he said to me, pouring a hefty measure into a straight glass, ignoring the small bowled Martini glasses the champagne was usually served in. He chugged at the liquid, finishing the glass with ease and burping flamboyantly. He had a throaty laugh and I found myself chuckling along too.

"Not a normal day at work though is it?" I said to him placatingly, pouring him another glass of champagne. The booze had seemed to loosen him up a little. He turned on his stool to face me.

"You got that right," he said "Usually I drive a boat tour but I took this gig for some extra money. With Christmas coming up I wanted to earn a little bit more for presents for my boy." He fished around in his pocket, bringing out a wallet and showing me a picture of a little boy in one of those portraits taken at school. He was proudly showing off a prominent gap of his front teeth in a big smile, his eyes crinkled in mirth.

"That's my Levi," the bouncer said, fatherly pride evident in his voice and his own smile a mirror image of the boy's, though with a few more teeth, "Fuck it. I'm not going to stay here," he said, looking at the picture of his son "They don't pay me enough to stay and look after the tourists over my own kid. No offence," he said, looking up at me again.

"None taken," I assured him "But can I come with you?"

The atmosphere in the room was now teetering on self destruction. I saw a couple of the dancers pulling on their outside coats. The woman who had danced for me not more than a hour ago came up to me, pulling the collar of her coat up around her ears.

"We're coming too," she told me, beckoning the small group of women behind her. She said it definitively, brooking no argument. Not that she'd get one from me.

The bouncer and I looked and each other. He shrugged nonchalantly. That seemed like enough of an agreement to me. I nodded at her and she beckoned us away from the bar, through a door at the back of the stage and down a long corridor. We passed the girl's changing room, heady with perfume and the slightly less pleasant undertone of old sweat. Through the open door I could see messy work-stations covered in makeup and accessories, one with a recently washed pair of tights hanging over the mirror, the feet of which were dripping steadily onto the floor. We went down a flight of stairs and the women in front of me pushed the bar of the emergency exit, depositing us out on the street. Management had obviously not thought to barricade that door which was worrying. But I wasn't complaining. Gulping at the air, I luxuriated in its cold freshness, not heavily tainted with cologne, perfume, spilled alcohol and pheromones.

"Emma" the women introduced herself to me, shaking my hand with a firm grasp as she gathered her coat around her skimpy outfit with the other. "Come" she instructed me. Glad of her confidence our misfit little group struck off into the city.

The figure made their way down the gang plank from the boat. Closing the one eye that was still (reasonably) open and crossing my fingers behind my back, I hoped and wished that it was a person, a normal, regular human person. Opening my eye again I noted that they seemed to be dressed in the smart uniform whites of cruise liner personnel. My heart lifted a fraction of an inch. Maybe they'd seen us cycling round the side of the ship and had opened up the gangplank to invite us in to safety. Maybe this guy would usher us into the secure opulence of a high class cruise ship and unleash us all on the teeming buffet. We could stuff crabs legs and blinis into the yawning chasms that had once been our stomachs. I licked my lips absent mindedly, the shrivelled sock of my stomach burbling loudly. The man turned to us, one arm swinging free of its socket, slapping against his thigh like a loose sleeve. The side of his uniform was stained and stiff with old blood from the tear in his neck and shoulder. I sighed. There would be no bottomless brunch for us, but maybe there would be for this guy if we weren't careful.

The creature registered our presence through eyes that had already started to cloud. It snarled in greeting and began making its shambling way down the gangplank. The thing moved in a disjointed hobble, like a ravenous marionette that had broken its strings and come to life. The hand on its good arm reached out for us, the fingers flexing open and shut, grasping for us. It cried out, guttural and wordless, but something answered it from somewhere deep inside the bowels of the ship.

I wanted to close my eyes again. I was so tired, utterly spent. I didn't think I had it in me for another showdown, and to what end? Even if we could fight this one off, how many more were there in the ship? Looking at the size of the vessel it could be in the thousands. What then? There would only be more and more and more until one of them got their teeth into me and I joined their shambling, ravenous ranks. What was the point in delaying the inevitable? I might have cried if I'd not been so dehydrated. My tear ducts burned mutinously as I rubbed at my face.

"Oh Shit. Shitting Shit it," I heard Brad yell in exasperation, followed by the hollow smack of something hard hitting flesh.

I pulled my hand away from my face in time to see the lone shoe from the terminal bouncing off the dead man's face. Brad was a cracking shot. It was a shame all that was to hand was junk and litter.

What I would have given for a slingshot or even a really pointy stick. Seeing Brad literally shifting through piles of crap in order to survive got me moving. I couldn't give up yet.

Turning away from the advancing dead, Meg and I made our way into the ferry terminal to look for something to defend ourselves with. The plumes of smoke from whatever now charred morsel that had been left in the sandwich shop's oven were almost choking. I swam through them to make my way back there. Strewn amongst the abandoned sliced cucumbers and shredded carrots were a couple of knives. They didn't look very sharp, but they'd probably be more use than a shoe or a smashed snow-globe. Picking up as many implements as I could manage in my pulverized hands I made my way back outside.

The broken marionette of a sailor had been joined by a deluge of chums, all with some form of mangling to their once vulnerable human bodies. I'd never even broken a bone before. It was hard to fathom how susceptible the human body was or how easy it was to subject it to this level of obliteration. I didn't know how most of the bodies coming at us were still standing. Some of them weren't but were intent on dragging themselves across the ground, bits of skin coming away, smearing across the floor like a road rash in slow motion. I threw the pitiful amount of scavenged utensils out to the members of the group. The bread knife I lobbed sailed over Ian's head and outstretched hand and clattered into the detritus . He skittered along after it, desperate for any kind of protection against the advancing hoard.

A tight knot of sailors made their way down the gangplank. One of them had the shortened gait and squishy sound of someone walking on a stump where a foot used to be. They rattled together like pool balls in a triangle in their haste to beat each other to dinner. The gangplank clattered, the metal on metal sound like the screech of fingernails on a chalkboard, as the melee of seamen tottered their way onto the mainland. In the darkness of the ship's mouth I saw the advancing shadows of the rest of its passengers. So much for hearing some wicked beat poetry from Derek. The combined force of the herd of creatures on the gangplank was making it shudder, the metal squealing as it moved against the pavement. There was no polite queuing system as the creatures rushed out from the bowels of the ship, desperate for some of the local cuisine. Instead of bitterballen or croquettes they were jonesing for the flesh of our small group.

"THE GANGPLANK!" Brad yelled from somewhere behind me.

I watched as it bounced and screeched, moving erratically with every footstep upon it. It had obviously not been secured when the ship docked. It had probably been released by someone trying to escape. Next to the open door was a small mound of bodies, tripping up the less agile creatures as they exited. Maybe one of them had managed to get it down before being overwhelmed. It didn't help me, I still didn't understand what Brad meant. I looked back at him, shrugging wildly, angry at him for not being more clear.

"THE GANGPLANK!" he reiterated, gesturing frantically at the boat with the vegetable peeler I had thrown to him.

It was probably one of the only times I had really wanted a man to explain something to me in painfully explicit detail. I had no idea what he expected of me. He might as well have been shouting "THE WINDOW!" or "THE WALL!" or "JON BON JOVI!" for all the relevance I could see in our current situation.

Before I could shout to him for further clarification he ran past me towards the boat, towards the crowd of creatures milling on the pavement like confused tourists. He came at them from an angle, trying to avoid their grabbing hands, and began pushing at the railing of the gangplank.

The metal squalled in protest against the pavement as Brad put his whole weight behind his push. It jumped a few inches, coming perilously close to the edge of the dock and the murky water below. I finally understood. If he could push the gangplank away from the dock, then the rest of the creatures on the boat wouldn't be able to disembark. Maybe they would fall straight into the water one after the other, like lemmings, to just bob around on its surface like discarded bottles or crisp packets. Michael seemed like he'd understood Brad's intentions far quicker than I had. He followed behind and helped Brad push the heavy structure. The creatures roared, brought to a fever pitch by tasty titbits in grabbing distance. Their hands sought out the boys, gripping at their clothes, faces, hair and limbs, trying to drag them over the railing towards them.

I stood stock still and watched them. I kept watching as Tim joined them, and then Ian. I saw the way the veins popped out on their necks as they heaved at the metal structure, how the pulsing of their blood so nearby stirred the blood lust in the creatures. They sped up, swarming out of the boat, creating a circle with the boys at their nucleus. The boy's line of escape was getting smaller and smaller, as the creatures figured out how to get to them. They continued to push, with the creatures in front of them and the water to their backs, their plight looking perilous. With a final, almost animal squawk, the gangplank lost its tentative grasp of the pavement and toppled sideways into the frigid waters with a splash, sending the creatures who were still crossing into the water with it. They bobbed and splashed but their bodies, filling with cold water from holes and gaps and bites, began to drag them down. Their dead weight was too much for bodies lacking any kind of fine motor skills. They began to sink, their grasping hands slipping under the murk. I wanted to yell, to whoop and punch the air in celebration but my jubilant mood was short lived.

Over the sounds of frantic splashing was the sound of Brad howling Michael's name. I hadn't seen him pitch into the water with the thrashing creatures, as the gangplank fell. Michael managed to cry out in the water, before it lapped into his open mouth drowning his screams. The creatures closest to him ignored their own buoyancy issues, in their bid to grab onto him and sink their teeth into his soggy flesh. They swarmed and dragged him under so quickly I might have only imagined him there. The water turned red and I knew it had been true. Michael was gone. He'd sacrificed himself as I had stood and watched. Brad cried out again, getting ready to dive in to save his friend. But there was no point. It was over.

Joe pushed past me, seemingly ready to dive into the scrum to help. I grabbed at his wrist, trying to hold him in place. He looked back at me with beseeching eyes but didn't pull his arm out of my grasp. The creatures finally reached Brad, Ian and Tim, falling on them in an ecstasy of feeding. Behind them, more creatures careened from the open door, falling into the water one after another. Their splashing and moaning almost drowned out the screams of Brad, Ian and Tim. Almost.

Leaning back against the building, I could feel the cold of the glass cubes seeping through my torn clothes into my tired body. It wouldn't be long. There were so many creatures on the shore already and only so much food to go around. As soon as they had finished with Brad and Tim, I knew the rest of us would be next. Gripping the knife tighter, I was glad of the pain from my damaged hands, glad to feel my body for this moment. I stretched, feeling all of my aching muscles protesting and luxuriated in it. I knew the next time I felt pain, it would be from the multitudes of teeth sinking into me, wrenching me limb from limb as I screamed the last seconds of my life away. I closed my good eye. I didn't want to see them coming.

"YOO HOO!" my eyes flew open again. Was I going mad? Maybe my brain was going haywire once faced with its own demise, creating auditory hallucinations.

My head whipped back and forth, searching for the source of the sound. Surely there was no way the creatures, still seemingly busy with their meal, were halloing us? I hadn't heard them make any other noise but chewing and snarling. I didn't think they could talk, let alone be friendly. It must be a hallucination. My mind was sluicing away from reality to try save my last conscious thoughts.

"COOEE!" came the same voice again.

Searching the faces of all of the creatures, I tried to make out which one was trying to get my attention. No-one was waving a hanky at me coyly to direct my gaze. I tried not to focus too long on their masticating jaws, on the small group gathering handfuls of flesh into their mouths from Tim, whose foot was still twitching from the last firings of his synapses.

Meg made her way out of the terminal behind us, clutching a pair of kitchen tongs and a stapler to her chest. At the scene in-front of us she grabbed onto my hand, letting the ineffective tools clatter to the floor.

"YE-HOO, JOOOEEEE," came the yell again.

"What the fuck?!" Joe breathed next to me, as confused as I was about the source of the noise.

At least if he was hearing it too then it wasn't the last vestiges of my sanity dribbling away. Was it? We stood together on the dock, straining to hear the next exaltation. In the distance, the sound of a steadily chugging motor was getting closer and closer. I shielded my eyes from the last embers of the sun in the sky. Round the corner, came one of the wide canal tour boats, sailing steadily towards us. At the front of the boat stood a man with an enormous belly, waving maniacally. Behind him stood several women, scantily dressed, some waving, some standing stoically watching us. A man dressed all in black, looking suspiciously like a bouncer, was steering the boat towards us. The creatures had not been distracted by our would be rescuers. Having run out of prone sustenance, they were beginning to advance on Joe, Meg and I.

"JUMP!" the rotund man yelled.

We all ran towards the water and the boat. The creatures reached for us, lunging like big cats come feeding time at the zoo. Meg disappeared from my peripheral vision, snagged by one of the creatures. I heard her body hit the pavement, listened to her scream but didn't stop running. I couldn't. I'd seen what happened to anyone who tried to help someone else – Stuart, John, Tommy, Brad, Tim – all of them eaten. My thighs burned as I willed them to just keep going, to please not give up on me quite yet. You know that bit in the action movie when the main guy has to do an impossible jump? The camera slows down to watch their heroic leap, that they make easily even though it's probably twenty feet and its followed up by some swelling crescendo from the soundtrack? Well, as I jumped I did indeed feel time slow down, the side of the boat came closer and closer, but I landed probably about eighteen feet short of my target.

The sting of my inelegant bellyflop and the slap of the cold water hit me all at once. It was like being punched by a block of cement. My head went under the surface, filling my mouth with the foul tasting water as I gasped. It was like swallowing (and inhaling a little bit) of a whole tin of tuna, brine and all. I surfaced quickly, spluttering on the horrible taste and coughing up the water from my lungs. Blinded by the water in my eyes I could only thrash blindly towards the sound of the boat and its passengers screaming at me to hurry up. Kicking my legs as hard as possible, I was terrified that a dead, waterlogged hand was going to grab my ankle and pull me down to the murky depths and the waiting teeth of the creatures at any moment. Who knew how long they could survive under the water? I'd seen drowned ones in the canal, sure, but had no idea how long they'd been under the water.

My clothes were getting heavier and heavier as they took on more water and my shoes seemed to weigh a tonne. I doggy paddled, blind and weighed down, splashing and thrashing until I bumped up against the side of the boat. It was far too high and I was far too tired to pull myself up onto the deck.

I thought that was it. I'd made it right to the finish line over to trip over the ribbon and crack open my skull on the podium. I was so close to safety and now I was going to drown. Fucks sake. My head dipped under the water and panic bobbed me back up like a cork. As the last of the strength leached from my arms I felt rough hands in my armpits, dragging me up and over the side of the boat where I lay gasping and flapping like a caught fish. Brackish water leaked from the side of my mouth into a little puddle on the deck. Over the sound of my ragged breathing, I heard jubilant shouting and back slapping. Joe was crying and telling the big man how happy he was that he'd made it. Neither of them seemed to be in a hurry to make any introductions, so I kept my eyes closed and tried to breathe in and out through my nose. I listened to their voices, floating above me, undulating in volume as they walked around.

"Where have you been?" I heard Joe ask.

"Mate you wouldn't believe it. After we left the strip club we had to go pick up Liam's son and that's where it got really crazy.....so you know.............and then when we got there Emma found a chainsaw. It was gross.........so gooey!.......We had to break into a shopping centre for new clothes. OK but hang on. This is the craziest bit........."

The drone of their conversation was oddly soothing as the boat chugged along below me, threatening to lull me to sleep or more likely unconsciousness. Who knew how long it had been since I last slept? The sensation of being watched prickled my skin. Rolling my head to the side I sluggishly opened the eye that still could obey my demands. Sitting on the edge of a moulded plastic seat was a large, bald man in the customary all black outfit of a bouncer. He was considering me with discerning brown eyes. Beside him sat a little blond boy, who cracked a wide gappy smile as I looked over to him and waved delightedly. The man had a proprietorial hand on his shoulder. I grinned back at the little boy, whose smile was infectious and gave a little shake of my own hand on the deck, not having the energy to lift it any higher.

"Alright?" the man in black said to me, seeming to relax a little as I smiled and waved at what must have been his son.

"Peachy," I said to him, rolling my head back into place in its puddle and closing my good eye again.

CHAPTER TWENTY-FOUR: JONAH

It feels good to tell everyone about Keith. My old friend, who turned out to be the hero of the hour, had some stories to tell us once we were safely onboard. The memory of him gesticulating wildly while recounted them makes me laugh. He didn't want to leave the strip club because he didn't think he could cope but his time in Amsterdam seemed far wilder than ours and I knew that, without him, neither myself or Jennifer would be here today. Once we were clear of danger Liam had docked the boat and we had made our way, together, to the airport where the army were waiting for us. Michael and Brad had been right after all. The army took our names, took our pictures and directed us to a gate at the airport where a plane was ready to take survivor's back to the UK.

Before I'd gone into the airport I looked back at Keith's little group. Emma, Liam, Levi and the others were nationals, they would be helped by the army in country. Keith had decided to stay. He had formed bonds that were stronger than nationality. I could see his arm sneak around Emma's waist, pulling her against his significant body. She looked up adoringly into his face, their love and trust for one another was almost gratuitous. I thought I should look away but I regarded them for a moment more, trying to gather all the details of them into my memory. I didn't know if I would ever see Keith again and I wanted this image to be my overriding memory of him.

Tears jump into my eyes as I think about Keith, our knight in shining armour looking into the eyes of his beloved. It seems a good point to end the story. No-one wants to hear about our trials and tribulations with the army before and after we disembarked our plane. No-one wants to hear what a terrible place that plane, full of badly traumatised and injured people was like (spoiler alert: not fun and not even a bag of peanuts on board). Leaving the story with Keith and Emma feels like an almost happy ending or as close to a happily ever after as any of us could ever get.

The audience is silent for a moment. I wonder if they are going to start booing, or pelting me with rotten fruit. Silently Amelia stands up from her seat and begins clapping. The sound is lonely in the large auditorium and the smile on my face is pained. I don't want a pity clap. That's definitely worse than no sound at all, or even rotten food-based missiles. But one by one, members of the audience begin to stand and join her. The clapping gets louder and louder as more people join in. As the thunderous applause dies down, there is another

sound in the room. Previously masked by the noise
of the crowd, it shrieks into the quietening air.

CHAPTER TWENTY-FIVE: JENNIFER

The entire audience looks around at one another in confusion. Now that the clapping has abated (along with my annoyance that it is Joe and not myself that is receiving the standing ovation) the mechanical keening of dozens and dozens of phones is almost deafening in the room. I know that tone. I have heard it out loud once before and I hear it often in my nightmares. Rushing into the backstage area I pick up my bag, which is vibrating across the floor from the force of the same noise. With trembling hands I rummage around in its depths, trying to grab onto it. It dances out of my grasp a couple of times, out of my sweat slicked hands. I look at the screen, hoping against hope **'EMERGENCY ALERT – EXTERNAL THREAT TO LIFE. SEEK SHELTER. AWAIT FURTHER INSTRUCTIONS'.** *No. No. No. Not Again. Please. I can't. I CAN'T.*

It takes everything I have, every inch of resolve to make it back out onto the stage. My legs feel like they don't belong to me anymore. Joe is staring at his own screen, his face completely devoid of colour. Under the stage lights he looks like a spectre. His mouth is moving in a constant mantra of denial. This can't be real. Surely it's some awful, tasteless prank from the organisers. I can't have gotten out of Amsterdam, for so many people to have died to get me out of there, to make it home and die here instead. It's got to be a cruel joke. For all of my big talk about the things you should have with you and the things you should do to stay safe, I have none of them with me tonight. I brought my best bag and my nicest heels because it was just a talk. I have no satellite phone and no weapon. My bag holds a tube of lipstick, my caterwauling mobile phone and a tampon that has come out of its packaging, picking up all of the lint from the bottom of my bag.

Stumbling down the steps of the stage I make my way to the curtains covering the bank of windows. I put my hand on the icy glass, hoping it will ground me somewhat. The view out of the auditorium window is of blossoming carnage. The cold, wet, London night is awash with people running. Dashing across the roads, dodging traffic, darting down into the dark mouth of the tube entrance across the street. Running and screaming. From up here they look like a murmuration of birds, swooping and sweeping, drawn by something unknowable. But I know what is scattering them. I can see one in the crowd now, running in a way that no human would ever run; throwing themselves forward at full speed on the slick pavement, arms loose and teeth gnashing. It falls, sliding into the retreating crowd like a bowling ball, knocking down people in a tumble of arms and legs. I can hear the shrieking through the windows. The distant wail of sirens and victims is blending into a haunting cacophony. Even from up here I can see blood on the pavement as the thing thrashes and gnaws, tearing into the tumbled crowd. A cry surges up my throat and expands in the dark space of the auditorium. Panic rushes up into its place. I pinch the skin of my forearm hard, hoping it will wake me from this nightmare, but my fingernails dig ragged shapes into my skin with no effect.

Joe comes up beside me, looking at the scene out of the window. Our combined, exhaled terror fogs the pane of glass. The sudden warmth of a person next to me makes my skin shrivel in revulsion and fear. I study his face as he takes in the scene outside and the ungodliness of the situation twists his features. The crowd from the auditorium gathers behind us, desperate to see the horror show playing out in the road below. Soon the entirety of the crowd seems to be pushing into my back, and my nerves scream out in disgust. It's too close. It's too much. It is too familiar. I slither out of their grasp and climb onto the stage, trying to jump start my brain out of its squalling, panicked loop of denial and into some semblance of survival mode.

From somewhere downstairs there is the tinkling

of breaking glass, the surprised yowl of someone caught unawares. They are inside.

The sound pushes the crowd into a frenzied terror. They turn, almost as one entity, like a school of fish, and begin to streak down the aisles towards the door topped with green, glowing emergency exit signs. I try to shout, to make myself heard over the panicked din, to tell them to not go that way, that down to the foyer is where death is waiting for them. Joe hears me. He grabs onto my arm and nods that he has understood.

"Go. Go. Go," I yell at him.

We fight our way through the crowd, like salmon trying to swim upstream, and both slam into the double doors, pushing both shut. The safety bar clicks home with a satisfying clonk. I push my back onto the doors and face the rest of the crowd still inside. Some are screaming at me to get out of the way. Some are crying and asking me what to do. It's deafening and I can't hear myself over them. I can't think. I don't know what to do. Don't make me. Not again. Please.

I look over to Joe. He is leaning against the other panel. The pretty woman I saw shouting to him from the audience is under his arm. He holds onto her protectively, trying to keep her from the crush of the audience. He looks over to me desperately, asking me with the shrug of his shoulders and his wide eyes what we should be doing. Shit. He doesn't know either. Before I can say anything to him, the wood I am leaning against begins to shudder and shake in its frame. I can feel each individual hammering of fists in my back and shoulders. I don't know whether it is the crowd trying to get back in to safety, or the creatures trying to get to the plethora of tasty morsels within. The feeling is so familiar and yet so unsettling that the hot squirt of saliva jumps in to my mouth once again. My vision goes woozy, and I think I can hear Ross calling to me, begging me to him back in.

CHAPTER TWENTY-SIX: JONAH

The panic in the room at the sound of breaking glass below us is almost a sentient thing. I can feel it wailing and thrashing somewhere in my chest. Amelia. In my rush to get to her I push people out of the way, harder than I should, but my fear has made me reckless and aggressive. I scoop her into the space under my armpit, where she sleeps against me night after night. I can feel the butterfly fluttering of her heart against me through our clothes. I pull her along with me, down the narrow aisle with the jostling crowd. They are as frightened as cows being sent down the chute at a slaughterhouse.

I pull the door closed as some of them try to squeeze out into the stairwell, to run blindly into the foyer and into the waiting arms of the predatory things waiting down there in the darkness, bloodstained and ravenous. I throw the weight of mine and Amelia's body against the door and lean against it. The corralled crowd roars in my face, desperate to be released. I use my body to try and shield Amelia from its wrath. I thought I'd had my fill of heroics but I can't move away. I can't let death in.

Jennifer is leaning against the door on the other side. We are the only things between the panicked crowd and the death that stalks the halls beyond.

"What's happening?" Amelia asks against my neck. I close my eyes. I don't want to release the words out into the room, to make their presence real, even though I have seen them out of the window.

"Them," I whisper into her hair. She smells like the coconut shampoo that sits on the side of our bath. She smells like home.

The hammering starts almost immediately. The decision that haunts me everyday is playing out again. Maybe I never made it back from Amsterdam. Maybe this is Hell and I am stuck in a loop of punishment. My version of Hell is being faced with the same choices around and round, watching people die ad infinitum. My Hell is having to decide whether to open a door over and over and over again. It is the grey places between black and white decisions.

"She made it you know," Amelia says, looking into my face.

"Who?"

"Kate. She spent a week in the coffee-shop on her own but the Army found her and got her out. She lived. Staying where she was meant she lived."

It dawns on me that Amelia knows more than she ever let on. All those nights bathed in the blue light from her iPad, she was piecing together as much information as she could find. Like a detective. She knew who Jennifer was when she showed me the page. She knew that if she showed me the advert I would book it. Amelia was trying to get me to face what happened out there. She was trying to do the best for me. I realise that she does know me. Really knows me. The man I was, the man I came back as. She knows every part of me. Now I have to make a decision. Do I open the door and rescue the living or hold them shut to stop the dead, sacrificing those already outside? Do we try to make our escape, right now or stay put and await rescue? Do I make the same decision or a different one this time? I look into Amelia's eyes and see the answer written large in them. I take a deep breath. I hold it. Here goes.

One.

Two.

Three.

ABOUT THE AUTHOR

Melanie Atkinson is a horror author living on the South coast of the UK with her husband and dog. She has been published in numerous short story anthologies in the UK, USA and Australia.

Find out more about the author at:

Website: https://melatkinsonwriter.wordpress.com

Instagram: melaniewriting

Twitter: 0mel_atkinson0

9 781738 445905